Rifle rounds followed Bolan

They kicked up dirt and grass all around him, lodging in the tree trunk as he popped back to his feet behind the pine tree.

Bolan stared in the moonlight, following the angle of the shots back to a man who stood partially out of the guard shack, wielding an M-16.

He aimed, pulled the trigger of his gun and sent two rounds into the guard's shoulder, causing him to drop his weapon. A look of shock covered the man's face for an instant before Bolan squeezed the trigger again, and the man fell out of the shack onto the pavement.

Bolan leaned out from around the tree trunk and sighted down the barrel. A lone round took out the second man at the gate. The third sentry was still hiding inside the small building, covered from the waist down by concrete but visible through the glass in the top of the window.

He aimed at the man's head and pulled the trigger. His slug struck the glass then ricocheted off with a loud whine. The window was bullet resistant—but *nothing* was completely bullet *proof.*

Bolan left the cover of the tree and raced toward the open door of the shack. The final sentry was squatting with his gun in hand, looking straight at him as Bolan fired his weapon. In the end, all of the concrete and bullet-resistant glass in the world hadn't helped him, and the guard fell on his face just as dead as the others.

The yard grew silent. Then, in the distance, Bolan heard sirens and he knew that the fighting had raised alarms.

The Executioner had to get away. Fast.

MACK BOLAN ®
The Executioner

The Executioner®
Don Pendleton's

DAMAGE RADIUS

A GOLD EAGLE BOOK FROM
WORLDWIDE®

TORONTO • NEW YORK • LONDON
AMSTERDAM • PARIS • SYDNEY • HAMBURG
STOCKHOLM • ATHENS • TOKYO • MILAN
MADRID • WARSAW • BUDAPEST • AUCKLAND

Recycling programs
for this product may
not exist in your area.

First edition December 2011

ISBN-13: 978-0-373-64397-4

Special thanks and acknowledgment to
Jerry VanCook for his contribution to this work.

DAMAGE RADIUS

Printed in U.S.A.

The laws are silent in the midst of arms.
                    —Marcus Tullius Cicero
                    106 BC–43 BC

I will go around the law to catch the bad guys, if I have to.
And I will break the law to stop them, if all else fails. I will
do what needs to get done—whenever, wherever, however.
                    —Mack Bolan

THE
MACK BOLAN
LEGEND

Nothing less than a war could have fashioned the destiny of the man called Mack Bolan. Bolan earned the Executioner title in the jungle hell of Vietnam.

But this soldier also wore another name—Sergeant Mercy. He was so tagged because of the compassion he showed to wounded comrades-in-arms and Vietnamese civilians.

Mack Bolan's second tour of duty ended prematurely when he was given emergency leave to return home and bury his family, victims of the Mob. Then he declared a one-man war against the Mafia.

He confronted the Families head-on from coast to coast, and soon a hope of victory began to appear. But Bolan had broken society's every rule. That same society started gunning for this elusive warrior—to no avail.

So Bolan was offered amnesty to work within the system against terrorism. This time, as an employee of Uncle Sam, Bolan became Colonel John Phoenix. With a command center at Stony Man Farm in Virginia, he and his new allies—Able Team and Phoenix Force—waged relentless war on a new adversary: the KGB.

But when his one true love, April Rose, died at the hands of the Soviet terror machine, Bolan severed all ties with Establishment authority.

Now, after a lengthy lone-wolf struggle and much soul-searching, the Executioner has agreed to enter an "arm's-length" alliance with his government once more, reserving the right to pursue personal missions in his Everlasting War.

1

Mack Bolan, aka the Executioner, lowered his left elbow slightly, stopping a right jab to the ribs from his left-handed opponent. He countered with a quick right cross which was also blocked. Slowly, the two men circled, sizing each other up and looking for weaknesses in the other's defense. A fierce left hook came suddenly toward the Executioner's face but he ducked under it, bobbing slightly to the side. In his mind, it registered that the southpaw he faced had dropped his left shoulder before delivering the blow. As well, Bolan realized the man had telegraphed the hook the same way each time he'd tried that punch.

The left hook was obviously the man's favored attack, and the pressure Bolan had felt when it landed on his arms told him it was powerful. Full of strength, and speed, the man could easily knock out an opponent if it landed solidly.

So, the soldier decided, it was time to set the man up and take advantage of his "tell."

Bolan backed away slightly, letting his opponent move closer. He ducked a wild right-handed "haymaker," then bobbed under another jab that followed it. Then, intentionally raising his left, he opened up his rib cage for the hook he hoped to draw from the other man.

It worked as if by magic.

Sweat poured from the other man's face as he dipped his shoulder in preparation to launch the hook.

Bolan didn't give him the chance. Stepping in swiftly, he dealt his opponent a powerful overhand right, which nailed the man squarely in the middle of the forehead. The man stumbled backward. Bolan shuffled closer again, jabbing a left into the man's midsection, which caused him to drop both of his hands.

It was time to end this fight.

Bolan put everything he had—arm, shoulder and a twist of the right hip—into the right cross.

His opponent was out before his face hit the canvas.

Quickly, Bolan stepped forward, saw that the man was breathing, then turned toward the ropes that encircled the boxing ring. Everyone else in the gym had halted their workouts in order to watch the match, and they stared up at Bolan with a mixture of surprise and newfound respect in their eyes. Bolan walked to the edge of the ring and rested his gloved hands on the top rope.

"Okay," he said. "I know you guys liked the former manager of this gym. I did, too. But he's dead, and there's nothing any of us can do about that." He paused, then motioned toward the unconscious man on the floor. "Jake, here, challenged me because all of you wanted to know if I knew what I was doing." He turned his head to include more men who had come to the ring on the other sides of the canvas. "Is there anyone here still wondering?" When there was no response from the spectators, Bolan went on. "Come on. I'm just getting warmed up. If there's anyone else who wants a piece of me, now's your chance."

The silence that had fallen over the gym didn't change, and no one took the Executioner up on his offer.

It soon became obvious that there would be no more challengers. "Then get back to your training, all of you," he said.

Lifting the top rope, he stepped under it before dropping to the gym's concrete floor. Using his teeth, he untied the lace on his right glove, then pulled it free and tucked it under his arm as he went to work on the left.

As he began unlacing the other glove, Bolan's eyes skirted the gym, taking in the men of various ages, sizes and abilities who had returned to the speed bags, heavy bags, double ended striking balls, jump ropes and other equipment. Most of them were innocent, honest fighters who were doing nothing more than trying to achieve their own personal dreams of success in the ring. But, unknowingly, they were actually part of one of the most extensive criminal organizations operating in the United States.

The Executioner eyed them again as he wiped a single drop of sweat from his brow with his forearm. This was only the starting point for the mission he had undertaken. And he was certain to engage in many more fights as he worked his way toward the goal of taking down Tommy McFarley's criminal organization.

But there was one point about the fight he had just won that stood out in the Executioner's mind as unique.

It was likely to be the only skirmish with rules, without weapons and without blood.

The Executioner was going to war yet again.

2

As the rat-tat-tat of the speed bags filled his ears like machine-gun fire, Bolan walked from the ring to the glass wall of his new office. Tossing the gloves he had just removed to a man on his way to the water fountain, he pushed the door open and left the gym proper. Through the glass, he could still hear the speed bags, the crunching of the canvas bags and the tapping of jump ropes as the door swung closed behind him.

The Executioner looked at his desk as he moved toward it. It was cluttered with the personal effects of Sy Lennon, the former manager of McFarley's New Orleans gym. But Lennon would not be back to collect them.

He, along with a middleweight named Bobby "the Killer" Kiethley, was dead. Their bodies had not yet been found, and Bolan suspected they never would be.

The rumor was that three of Tommy McFarley's henchmen had dropped them out of one of McFarley's private aircraft somewhere over the Gulf of Mexico. Their crime? Not throwing a fight that McFarley had "fixed," and upon which he had consequently lost close to a million dollars in bets.

Bolan spied an empty cardboard box thrown carelessly into the corner of the office and quickly retrieved it. Without ceremony, he used his forearm to sweep the desktop clear.

Papers, paperweights, a brass clip in the shape of a whale and a small plastic "Snoopy" wearing boxing gloves fell into the box. Returning the carton to the corner of the room, the Executioner dropped it and took a seat behind the desk.

For a moment, he stared out through the glass at the men still working out in the gym. New Orleans was the center of McFarley's operations, but his chain of boxing and body-building/power-lifting gyms stretched from the Atlantic to the Pacific. They were the "front," and the money-laundering operations, for his real businesses, which included international drug trafficking, arms dealing, gambling and white-slavery prostitution throughout the Western Hemisphere.

Bolan glanced at the scarred black rotary telephone that was now the sole object on his desk. It was a throwback to an earlier era, and the chances of it being tapped by McFarley were slim. Still, there was no sense in taking unnecessary risks, so the soldier leaned down to the gym bag he had dropped by the desk chair when he'd first arrived a few hours earlier. Fishing through the clothing and other contents, he found a smaller, zippered bag that contained both cell and satellite phones. Choosing the cell, he pulled it from the bag and tapped in the number to Stony Man Farm, the top-secret U.S. site that fielded counterterrorist teams and trained specially picked soldiers and police officers from America and its allied nations. The call was automatically routed through a number of cutout numbers on three continents on the off-chance that someone—someone like McFarley—had stumbled onto the frequency.

Barbara Price, the Farm's mission controller, answered the phone. "Hello, Striker," she said. "How's training?"

Bolan chuckled softly. "Barely worked up a sweat yet," he told the beautiful honey-blonde. He pictured her briefly in his mind. He and Price had a "special relationship" reserved for those rare occasions during which he was out of the field and spent the night at the Farm. But both were true professionals, and they never allowed that relationship to interfere with their work. "Had to prove myself a few minutes ago," Bolan went on.

"I doubt it lasted a full round," Price said.

"About a minute or so," the soldier replied. "I didn't see any reason to show off." He paused, then got to the point of the call. "Can you buzz me through to Hal?"

"I could," Price said. "But it wouldn't do you much good. He's at Justice today."

Hal Brognola wore two hats. In one role, he was the director of the Sensitive Operations Group, based at Stony Man Farm. But in another, he was a high-ranking official within the U.S. Department of Justice. "I'll call him there, then," Bolan told Price.

"Good luck and be careful."

"Always," he said and ended the call.

A moment later he had dialed the numbers to the big Fed's direct line at the Justice Department. A gruff voice answered. "Brognola."

"Striker here."

"Hello, big guy," Hal Brognola said after turning on the scrambler. "How's the new job?"

"Terrific," Bolan answered. "If you like starting at the bottom. I'm in, but I'm still a long way from McFarley's real action. Unless we can figure out a way to speed things up, it's going to take me a lifetime to get next to the man."

"You haven't met McFarley, himself, yet, have you?" Brognola asked.

"No," Bolan said. "I was interviewed and got hired by one of his goons. It seems the big man doesn't dirty himself with small jobs like hiring gym managers."

"Well," Brognola said, "I've got something else working right now that ought to lead to a meeting. The same undercover DEA agent who's managing McFarley's gym in Cleveland—the guy I went through to get you in there in New

Orleans—has let a few things 'slip' about your less-than-spotless past. It shouldn't take long for loose lips to reach McFarley's ears that you've run both guns and dope in the past, and that you're just trying to keep a low profile by managing boxers for a while."

"Your DEA man in Cleveland," Bolan asked. "How much does he know?"

"Not much. He's a good man. He understands the need-to-know concept and realizes he doesn't need to know anything past recommending you, alias 'Matt Cooper' of course, for the New Orleans job."

"You think this rumor-passing stunt is going to work?" Bolan asked.

"I think so," Brognola said. "Guys like McFarley are always on the lookout for men with Matt Cooper's experience."

A tap on the glass door to his office caused Bolan to look up. When he did, he saw a man wearing striped overalls and a tool belt, with a paint can in his hand. Bolan knew what he was there to do, and he nodded.

The man in the overalls set the can down, pulled a razor-bladed paint scraper from his tool belt and began scraping Sy Lennon's name off the glass door. In its place, he would paint Bolan's undercover ID—Matt Cooper.

"Okay," Bolan said, turning his attention back to the phone. "I guess all I can do right now is wait."

"It shouldn't take long," Brognola came back.

Without further words, Bolan disconnected the line.

He looked up again just in time to see a blurry form through the glass. It shoved the man in the overalls aside and pushed through the door.

Jake Jackson, the fighter the Executioner had KO'd only a few minutes earlier, strode angrily into the office. A cotton ball was shoved into his left nostril and flecks of dried blood still stuck to the skin around his nose. A welt was forming on his forehead between his eyes, and while he'd lost the boxing gloves from his hands, dirty-white tape was still wrapped around his palm and wrists.

"Something more I can help you with, Jake?" Bolan said as he set down the cell phone.

"Yeah," the man across the desk said. His lips were curved down in an angry frown, and his eyes shot daggers through Bolan. "I don't like getting whipped by a trainer," he growled.

Bolan glanced at the man's midsection. He was a heavyweight, but there was a thin layer of fat covering his abdominal muscles. "I don't blame you," the soldier said. "So if I was you I'd train harder, drink less beer and get into fighting shape."

The words only angered the man further. "I grew up here," he said in a heavy Cajun accent. "In the back streets of the French Quarter." He paused and eyed Bolan even harder. "And I can't help but think there'd be a much different outcome if you and I were to fight without gloves and rules." By this point Jackson had inched his way around the side of Bolan's desk.

The soldier swiveled slowly in his chair to face him. "There's only one way to find out, Jake," he said with a pleasant smile on his face.

The heavyweight lunged suddenly with both hands aimed at Bolan's throat. Still seated, the Executioner flicked his foot up and out, catching the other man squarely in the groin with the top of his flat-soled boxing shoes. The cup Jackson wore cushioned a lot of the blow, but not enough to keep him from grunting in surprise and pain.

As he rose from his chair, Bolan drove a forearm into the man's face. Blood spurted from the heavyweight's nose, shooting the cotton from his nostril like a tiny rocket and driving his head back upward. In his peripheral vision, Bolan saw that most of the other fighters had gathered around the glass front of the office to watch.

Jackson had obviously announced his intentions to "teach Matt Cooper a lesson" before he'd come into the office.

Bolan reached forward and clasped his hands together behind Jackson's neck. As he bent the man forward again, he drove a knee upward into his belly in a classic Muay Thai movement. Dropping his foot to the ground, he lifted his other knee and struck the groin area again.

By now, Jackson's plastic cup had cracked in two. And with the third knee strike, the fighter's groan became a scream.

Bolan stepped back and drove the same right cross into the man's chin that had knocked him out in the ring.

The effect was the same, and Jackson fell to the floor next to the desk.

Bolan didn't hesitate. Grabbing a handful of the man's sweaty hair with his left hand, he dragged him back around the desk and opened the door with his other hand. Then, pushing the unconscious man through the doorway, he let him fall on his face against the concrete.

The Executioner looked up. "I'm getting sick of this," he told the stunned fighters who had watched the encounter. "How many times do I have to knock this guy out? Let's get it all over with right now. I beat him in the ring, with rules. And I just beat him in a streetfight, without rules. Does anybody want to wrestle? Karate? Judo? Maybe do a little head-on tackling practice like in football?" He paused to let his words sink in. "Like I said, I'm through proving myself. If any of the rest of you want to fight, in any way you want, step up now." He paused again because he knew his next words would fall on the ears of his audience as the most important. "But I'm warning you," he finally said. "The next time, I'm going to *kill* my challenger."

The gym grew even more silent than it had been earlier.

Finally, a man who looked to be around welterweight size stepped forward. He had the coffee-colored skin of the true Creole, and was wearing sweatpants and bag gloves. He smiled at Bolan, then turned to face the other men. "I think it's high time we welcomed Mr. Cooper as our new manager," he said.

The rest of the heads nodded. Some enthusiastically, others grudgingly. But one way or another, they all affirmed Bolan's leadership.

The soldier nodded back to them also, then turned back into his office. A door at the rear of the room led to the small sleeping quarters that had served as Lennon's home, and would temporarily house the Executioner—at least during the beginning of this mission.

Just before he stepped into the small bedroom, Bolan glanced back over his shoulder.

The men around the gym were working out even harder than before. And the painter in the striped overalls was just beginning the second *T* in the name "Matt Cooper."

3

The call on the black rotary phone came just after the Executioner had ushered the last fighter out of the gym and locked the door behind him. Hearing it through the glass, he hustled around the ring in the center of the room, past a series of heavy bags and striking balls, and through the glass door into the office. "Cooper," he said as he pressed the old-fashioned receiver to his ear.

"How am I supposed to book fighters if you keep beating them up?" a laughing voice on the other end of the line asked in a thick Irish brogue.

Bolan knew it had to be McFarley. The man had immigrated to America from Northern Ireland, and still had his accent. But since it had been one of his underlings who had actually hired "Matt Cooper" to manage the gym, the Executioner pretended not to recognize the voice. "Who is this?" he asked.

"Your boss," McFarley said. "Your employer. Tommy McFarley, boyo."

"Well," Bolan said, "it's nice to finally talk to you."

"Did you have a specific conversational topic in mind, laddie?" McFarley said.

"Yeah," Bolan said. "How about a raise?"

McFarley laughed again. "I think I'm going to like you, Matt Cooper," he said. "You've got balls. But I hear you nearly left one of my heavyweights without his this afternoon."

"He was asking for it," Bolan replied.

"I know that particular fighter, and I have no doubt that was the case," McFarley said. "But that's not what I called about. A little bird told me there's more to you than just being a cauliflower-eared pug. You seem to have quite a résumé which you didn't mention to my man who hired you."

"It didn't seem relevant," Bolan said. "Besides, I'm trying to fly under the radar for the time being."

"When you're with me there's no radar problem," McFarley said. "I've got more radar detectors than Radio Shack."

"Great," Bolan said. "So…did you just want to remind me of how wonderful I am? Or is there some other reason behind this call?'

Yet again, McFarley burst into laughter. "You're a bold one, you are," he said. "I like that in a man." Then he stopped speaking, and when he started again his voice was far less jovial. "Up to a point."

Bolan remained silent.

"I'd like you to come join me for a late dinner," McFarley said.

"When?" the Executioner asked.

"Tonight," McFarley said. "I'm about to send a limo to pick you up right now. Can you be ready in thirty minutes?"

"Give me forty-five," Bolan said. "I've got to take a shower and change clothes."

"Forty-five it is then, laddie," the New Orleans crime kingpin said. "I look forward to meeting you."

Bolan heard the line click dead in his ear.

The Executioner looked at his watch as he walked back into his room. There was a small private bathroom attached, and he stepped into it, unlaced his high-topped boxing shoes, then stripped off the plain gray sweatshirt and gym shorts he'd been wearing with them. A moment later he had the shower running and warming up.

Bolan brushed his teeth, gargled, then glanced at his face. He had a five-o'clock shadow, but he decided to let it go. Tommy McFarley might be rich, but classy, he wasn't. And besides, the unshaved look seemed to be in fashion among the fighters at the gym and other young men he'd seen around lately.

Bolan showered quickly, then went to the short clothes-bar that ran the length of one side of the small room. He had moved in just that morning, and from the hangers he'd hung below the bar he pulled a navy-blue polo shirt, a pair of light tan slacks and a light brown sport coat, placing them on the bed as he pulled on plain white underwear and dark blue socks. The shirt and slacks went on next, then he stepped into a well-worn pair of brown loafers.

Reaching under the bed, the Executioner slid out a black, hard plastic case. A combination lock secured the case, and he dialed in the combination before opening the lid. Lifting the Beretta 93-R with the attached sound suppressor and the .44 Magnum Desert Eagle, he stared at the two weapons.

They had killed more men than he could remember. But all who had fallen to their rounds had deserved death, and more. A shoulder holster for the Beretta with two extra magazines on the other end of the straps, and a Concealex plastic hip holster that fit the Desert Eagle rested just under the guns. Bolan placed both weapons and their carriers to the side.

There would be a time for them, and the even heavier armament he had brought with him on this mission, later.

Lifting the bumpy foam rubber padding on which the guns had rested, Bolan dug through a variety of smaller pistols and knives on the layer below. His eyebrows lowered as he made his decisions, finally pulling out the stubby North American Arms Pug and a Cold Steel Espada folding knife. The minute single-action Pug revolver brought a faint smile to the Executioner's lips. The name seemed ironically appropriate for a man managing a boxing club. It held five rounds of .22 Magnum ammunition and was the best last-ditch backup he had ever found. It was smaller, and packed a better punch than the larger .22 LR or .25-caliber automatic guns on the market. Especially loaded as it was with hollowpoint bullets.

The Espada folding knife was a true blend of ancient Spanish tradition and modern technology. Patterned after the huge folding navajas that had been used in Spain for centuries—the newer Cold Steel version featured a "hook" opener at the base of the blade that allowed it to be drawn and opened on a pocket or waistband. It could be put into use faster than any switchblade, and when a natural front grip was taken, the nearly eight-inch blade had the reach of an eleven-inch bowie knife.

It was, quite simply, the finest folding fighting knife available.

Bolan clipped the Espada inside his waistband, against his kidney, then stared at the little .22 Magnum revolver in the palm of his left hand. He suspected that he'd be frisked before being allowed into this first meeting with McFarley, and he had no intention of disappointing whoever drew the job. He expected the Espada to be found, and was willing to sacrifice it as a diversion from the small firearm. But he also wanted to impress McFarley with his ability to move clandestinely through the search, and so he shoved the Pug down the front of his pants and placed it just under his groin between his underwear and slacks.

It would be painfully slow to retrieve from that position, but Bolan didn't expect any gunplay during this initial meeting with his target.

On this night, the NAA Pug .22 Magnum revolver would be more for show than fighting.

The Executioner shrugged into his sport coat, grabbed his

key ring from the top of the shabby wooden dresser in the tiny sleeping room, then moved back through the gym toward the front door.

The long black limousine pulled up to the curb as he locked the gym from the outside. The chauffer hurried out and opened the back door for him.

Without a word, Bolan slid inside.

McFARLEY HAD GROWN UP ON a small farm near Bushmill, Northern Ireland, which was the home of the world's oldest whiskey distillery—Old Bushmills. As a boy, he had worked the farm, sowing and reaping many of the grains that went into the whiskey being fermented only a few miles away. If he had learned one thing during that time, it was that the Bible was correct when it said, "That which you sow, so shall ye reap."

And as far as McFarley was concerned, that meant you reaped very little for the amount of backbreaking sowing that went into farming.

The Irishman sat back against his desk chair and glanced around the walls of his office. The wooden paneling was of the finest smooth cedar, and sent a soothing fragrance into the air of the room. The photographs and other documents that spotted the walls were framed in solid gold and silver. His desk was of the purest mahogany and teak. The fact was, everything in the room was the best money could buy.

But that money sure hadn't come from farming.

McFarley chuckled to himself as he dropped his desk phone back into its cradle. It would be a good hour still before Matt Cooper arrived for dinner, and he had only one other duty on his agenda that needed to be taken care of before the man arrived. The men with whom he needed to meet were already waiting for him in the outer office with his secretary, but the Irishman decided to let them wait a bit longer. They all needed to sweat a little, wondering exactly why they'd been called in to see him. So, while he let their anxiety rise, McFarley decided to take a few minutes to reminisce.

The Irishman let his mind drift back to his teenage days in Northern Ireland, when his only interests were boxing and women—not necessarily in that order. He had won Ireland's golden gloves heavyweight division four years running, then opened his own gym. But it had been around that time when he'd also gotten involved with the then very active PIRA— Provisional Irish Republican Army—the last faction of the IRA to quit bombing and shooting the British invaders. His interest in the organization, however, had not been political. He had found that more money could be made in one evening of smuggling guns, dynamite and C-4 or Semtax plastic explosives than he made in a year at his gym. Drug smuggling had come as a natural extension to his business, which meant even more money. And more money meant more women, so soon he had established a successful "call girl" service to supplement both his own seemingly insatiable urge for sex and his overall income.

It was about that time that Tommy McFarley realized just how small Northern Ireland really was. And that realization spawned his interest in immigrating to the U.S.

A frown crossed McFarley's face as he remembered his first attempts to gain his green card. It had not been as easy as he would have expected, since Great Britain was not considered to be a repressive nation—even to the Northern Irish. But a few clandestinely taken photos of a U.S. congressman visiting London—engaging in some rather unusual sex acts with two of McFarley's women —had convinced the man to push the Irishman's immigration papers through personally. And he had passed his citizenship test five years later with flying colors.

"Hurray for the red, white and blue." McFarley laughed out loud as the memory crossed his mind.

McFarley leaned back farther and clasped his hands behind

his head, staring at the various boxing trophies and other awards around the room. He had found, just like the Mafia and South American drug cartels before him, that energetic civic work was not only a good cover for his real pursuits, it endeared him to the people. And public opinion had a huge influence on politicians, be they senators, congressmen or district attorneys. The Irishman caught himself grinning again at a "Citizen of the Year" award on his wall from the New Orleans Chamber of Commerce.

There was not another city in the U.S. known for as much corruption and graft as the Big Easy. And Hurricane Katrina had disrupted things to an extent where bribes and leverage worked on the politicians and police even better than before the storm.

McFarley leaned back against his desk chair and chuckled aloud. What more could you ask for than television news footage that showed uniformed police officers pushing shopping carts through stores and looting them just like the rest of the citizenry? The Big Easy had become a Disneyland for criminals, so New Orleans had been the natural site for McFarley to base his operations.

Over the past few years those operations had been both legal and illegal. His string of weight-lifting gyms now rivaled both Gold's and World's, and each rep the "muscle heads" performed on the bench press or preacher curl stand put more money in his pocket. He also had boxing operations in most major cities across the country, and every punch that struck a bag or chin made him money as well. But these were fronts for his true revenue operations. His *real* money still came the "old-fashioned" way—he stole it. Although he, himself, was thoroughly insulated by several layers of employees, his illegal activities included gunrunning to the Shining Path in Peru and the FARCs in Colombia, call girl services and massage parlors in most major cities, and some blatantly outright brothels. Like the one he was presently sitting atop.

The penthouse of the old antebellum mansion, which faced Lake Pontchartrain, had been turned into McFarley's offices. There was little secrecy about what happened on the four floors below. Police and other cleanup workers—still trying after all these years to get the Big Easy up and running once more—had more pressing business than pursuing misdemeanor prostitution arrests.

The Irishman chuckled again. Besides, he thought, the top brass of the New Orleans PD and the district attorney's office were some of his best customers.

McFarley leaned forward, crossed his arms on the desktop and thought briefly about the one last thing he had to do before Matt Cooper arrived for dinner. Even thinking about performing such a task would have sent many men running to the restroom to throw up, but to McFarley, it seemed to come naturally. He had done similar things many times in the past, and he felt no emotion about them one way or another. It was all business, he thought, as his mind returned to his overall empire of crime once again.

In addition to the weaponry he sent south, he brought cocaine and heroin north into the U.S. for the Mexican and South American cartels. Of course, his favorite activity was still fixing boxing matches in the smoky clubs where his fighters fought. Although the gambling money he made from these fights was small compared to his profits in the other areas, he hung on to it as a nostalgic link to his past.

McFarley's smile turned suddenly downward. Once in a while, a fighter or his manager didn't go along with his wishes to take a dive. That had happened less than a week ago.

Which was why that fighter and his manager were no longer around. And never would be again. And why Cooper had been hired to take the manager's place, and was consequently on his way to the brothel to meet McFarley.

Slowly, and somewhat reluctantly—because part of him re-

belled against the racing technology taking over the world—
McFarley twisted his chair to the left and faced his computer.
He knew very little about the machines, but he had found
email to be an effective addition to his business. So, calling
up a message he had already read through once, he hit the
properties icon, set the computer to print in fast draft mode,
then hit Print.

A moment later, the printer sputtered to life and a single
sheet of paper came sliding out of the machine.

The Irishman looked up and down the page. He had used
one of his New Orleans PD contacts to have a background
check run on Matt Cooper. And as he stared at the page,
he saw that the man had been arrested for some of the very
crimes that were nothing more than a day's work for McFarley Enterprises. And these arrests had been effected all over
the world.

But there was one thing that impressed the Irishman far
more than the arrests. Matt Cooper had absolutely zero convictions. In fact, none of the crimes had even gone to trial. All
of which meant Cooper knew how to play the law, much as
McFarley did.

His reminiscing had come full circle, and McFarley decided it was time to finish the last item of business for the
day. Lifting the telephone again, he tapped on the intercom
and said, "Grace, send the men in, please. And you can go
home."

A moment later, the door opened and a square-shouldered
man lumbered in. His suit coat was too small, and it gaped
at the back of the neck. His crooked nose leaned to the left,
which tended to make him look cross-eyed. He had once been
a light heavyweight with over a hundred wins in the clubs.
But he had never come close to the big time. So when he'd
finally grown too old to fight, McFarley had given him a job
as one of his personal bodyguards. Looking back, McFarley
realized that had been a mistake.

Jo-Jo Gau was the man's name, and while he didn't know it yet, he was about to hit the canvas for the last time.

Gau was followed by two other men. Razor Westbrook and Felix O'Banion. O'Banion was a fellow Irishman who McFarley had brought to the U.S. when he was first establishing his operation. He had been a mediocre middleweight in Ireland but was smarter than the average fighter. Most of all, McFarley knew he was loyal and could be trusted.

The smaller Westbrook had fought a few fights in the featherweight division in the U.S. But like O'Banion and McFarley, he'd realized he would never be a champion on the professional level, and been smart enough to get out of the game before he'd damaged his brain.

The Irishman behind the desk felt his jaw tighten. O'Banion and Westbrook might not have been particularly good boxers, but they had proved they could pull the trigger of a gun with the best of them.

As the three men took seats on a couch across from McFarley's desk, the Irishman studied their faces. Westbrook and O'Banion looked slightly puzzled.

Gau was outright scared. And had every reason to be.

McFarley broke the silence. "You did a good job of getting rid of our two troublemakers," he said after the door had swung closed. His gaze moved to Gau. "But the problem goes deeper than those two men."

The three men on the couch shifted uncomfortably. Still staring at Gau, McFarley opened the desk drawer in front of him. He glanced down to see the pearl-handled Webley .455 revolver that he had brought with him from Ireland. It was still hidden from the men on the other side of the desk.

"The New Orleans gym falls under your care, Jo-Jo," McFarley said as he casually wrapped his fingers around the pearl grips of the wheel gun. "It was your responsibility to see that Kiethley took a dive."

Gau covered his mouth with a big fist and coughed nervously. "Boss," he said, "I did my best. They told me they were both cool with it."

McFarley stared at the man. *Gau.* Was it a French name? It sounded like it. Not that it mattered.

When he didn't answer, Gau began talking nervously again. "I was in the dressing room with them right before the fight," he said in a slightly trembling voice. "They both swore Kiethley would go down in the third round." He coughed again. "Kiethley was going to wait on that jab-uppercut combination the other guy liked to use, let it land, then fall."

"But that's not what happened, was it?" McFarley said.

Gau's coughing became almost spasmodic. "No, sir," he managed to get out between the roars from his throat. "They lied. I don't know why. Maybe the other side paid them more than we were going to."

"That's really no excuse, Jo-Jo," McFarley said. "It's your responsibility to see that things like that don't happen."

"I know, boss." Gau coughed out once more. "And it won't happen again. I swear it won't."

"There's no need to swear to it," McFarley said. "I'm going to personally make sure it doesn't ever happen again." He paused as his fingers tightened around the pearl grips of the Webley. "At least not on your watch."

Without another word, McFarley lifted the big revolver, aimed it at Gau's crooked nose and pulled the trigger.

The blast sounded like a nuclear bomb going off in the closed office. The .455-caliber lead bullet struck Gau between the eyes and he fell back against the couch, his arms dropping to his sides. The man's eyes stared wide-open at McFarley.

The nervous coughing stopped, but Gau's eyes still looked scared, even in death.

The sudden explosion had gotten Westbrook's and O'Banion's attention, too. They looked at McFarley, then Gau's corpse, then back to McFarley again. McFarley wouldn't have called their expressions shocked by any means;

they had seen him perform violent acts before with guns, baseball bats and other items. But neither had been expecting to witness a cold-blooded murder at this time.

McFarley dropped the Webley back into the drawer and shoved it closed. "Get rid of the body the same way you did the others," he said simply. "Drop him out of the plane somewhere between here and Cuba. The sharks need to eat just like every other animal on the planet."

Westbrook and O'Banion nodded and stood up. O'Banion grabbed Gau under the arms, and Westbrook took the dead man's ankles as they maneuvered him off the couch toward the door.

The telephone on the desk rang. McFarley answered it as the two men opened the door and began clumsily carting the former fighter out into the hall. "Yeah?" the Irishman said into the receiver.

"Tommy," a soft voice purred.

McFarley recognized the voice immediately. It belonged to Sugar, the madam who managed the brothel on the lower floors of the building. She was no longer a working girl herself—McFarley kept her for his own private use. Of course he didn't limit himself in that way, and in addition to her he had one or more of the other prostitutes several times a day. Sometimes with Sugar. Other times, alone.

"What is it, sweetheart?" McFarley said into the phone.

"Is everything all right?" Sugar asked. "We thought we heard a shot...." Her voice trailed off.

"Everything's fine, Sugar. Thanks for checking. Now, keep it warm for me and get the other girls back to work."

"All right, lover," Sugar purred and hung up.

By the time McFarley had replaced the receiver, Westbrook and O'Banion had toted the dead body from the room. The Irishman looked toward the couch and the wall behind it.

Blood and brain matter covered the expensive upholstery, and he started to call down to the janitor—a man who was vastly overpaid to keep the brothel clean and his mouth shut—to come up and clean the mess but then thought better of it. He doubted the stains would all come out even with the industrial strength cleaner the custodian used. So he made a mental note to send O'Banion out in the morning to buy a new couch.

McFarley looked down at his watch. Matt Cooper would be here soon, and an idea suddenly struck him. He could use the gory mess on the couch and wall as an object lesson to this potential replacement for Gau. He could bring the new gym manager up here to his office after dinner. Let him see for himself what happened to McFarley's employees when they screwed up.

The Irishman stood up and found himself nodding. An excellent idea, he decided, as he rounded his desk and left his office. He walked down another hall to his private living quarters. As he opened the door, the faint-but-familiar odor of perfume filled his nostrils. McFarley smiled as he walked through the living room to the bedroom.

Sugar had known he'd be wanting her as soon as she had heard the shot. She was a smart woman—especially for a whore—and she knew the types of activities that made men's testosterone levels rise.

So there she was, already lying back on the bed, wearing a smile.

And nothing else but a red garter belt, matching fishnet hose and five-inch heels.

4

It was half-past-eight when the limo driver pulled through the iron gates and halted in front of the mansion. He hurried around the automobile to open Bolan's door. As he stepped out of the vehicle, the smell of salt water hit him in the face and the soldier remembered that Lake Pontchartrain was second only to the Great Salt Lake as America's largest inland body of salt water.

The driver escorted him up the steps, through two rows of chiseled marble statues in the forms of Greek gods, to the front door. The man pressed a button, and the melodious sound of two bars of music came from somewhere inside the huge mansion.

A moment later, a braless woman wearing a light, see-through shift through which a red garter belt and fishnet stockings were visible, opened the door. "Good evening, Mr. Cooper," she said in her best sultry tone. "Mr. McFarley is expecting you." She paused and stepped back to allow Bolan to enter. "My name is Sugar. It's because I'm so sweet."

"I don't doubt it a bit," Bolan said, smiling. He looked her up and down from head to toe, like he knew any hedonistic criminal such as the one he was portraying would do. "I hope I get a taste before the night's over."

A huge smile spread across Sugar's face. She was undoubtedly pleased by the compliment, but her words told Bolan it wasn't going to happen. "Sorry, honey," the scantily-clad woman purred. "But I'm Tommy's private stock."

Bolan effected a laugh. "Well, if you're not selling," he said, "you shouldn't advertise so well."

This comment seemed to please Sugar even more. But a moment later, she became more businesslike—at least as businesslike as possible being dressed as she was. "Please come with me, Mr. Cooper," she said. "Mr. McFarley is anxious to meet you." With that, she turned her back to Bolan and began an exaggerated wiggle-walk down a hallway to an elevator. Bolan glanced at her hips as she strutted on. She wore no underwear beneath the garter belt, and she swayed back and forth provocatively with every step.

When the elevator doors opened, Sugar stepped back and motioned Bolan to enter. "Just push *P* for penthouse, Mr. Cooper," she said, her words still dripping with sexuality. "A couple of Mr. McFarley's associates will be waiting for you."

Bolan did as instructed and watched the elevator doors roll closed again. As he rose in the car, he wondered when the device had been installed. The house itself looked to have been built long before the advent of elevators. At one time, it had probably been the main house that oversaw a large plantation near New Orleans.

The doors rolled open again and, just as Sugar had promised, there stood two men wearing dark suits and ties. A slight frown showed on both faces, and the mood suddenly shifted from Sugar's friendliness to a slightly dangerous feel.

Both of the men had scars at the corners or their eyebrows, a dead giveaway that they were former fighters. The smaller of the two stepped forward and said, "I'm sorry, Mr. Cooper, but we've got to frisk you before we let you go any farther."

Bolan had expected this, and as he stepped off of the elevator he extended both hands to his sides.

The man who had spoken started at Bolan's ankles and began running his hands up the outside of his legs, looking for weapons. When he reached the waistband of Bolan's slacks, his hand stopped on the Cold Steel Espada clipped inside. Pulling it from the Executioner's belt, his eyes widened when he saw the size of the knife. Using both hands, he opened the blade, then said, "What had you planned on doing with this monster, Mr. Cooper?"

"Anything I needed to," Bolan came back.

"You're a knife fighter, are you?" the slightly larger goon standing behind the man holding the knife asked. His voice was slightly sarcastic.

"I'm a fighter, period," Bolan said calmly.

The smaller man returned to Bolan's ankles. This time he began feeling through his slacks on the inside of his legs. Just before he got to the groin area, Bolan said, "You seem like a guy who really gets off on this kind of thing. You planning to think about me later tonight, when you're all alone in bed?"

The comment generated an instant homophobia in the searcher, and he barely tapped the Executioner's groin area before moving on up to check his chest, arms and shoulder. Satisfied, he said, "Looks like you're clean except for the pig-sticker." He paused, staring self-consciously up into Bolan's eyes. "You'll get it back when you leave." Those words ended in another short pause, until finally he said, "And no, I don't plan to think of you when I go to bed tonight. You're not my type."

"That's encouraging," Bolan answered.

Without further ado the two men turned and led Bolan down a somewhat confusing set of intertwining hallways until they came to an elaborately furnished dining room.

Tommy McFarley was on his feet, waiting, just outside the room.

The man who had taken Bolan's Espada whispered something into McFarley's ear, then he and his partner disappeared back down the hallway.

Bolan studied McFarley's face for a moment. The man looked slightly older than the pictures in the Stony Man file Bolan had reviewed during his flight to New Orleans. A little white had begun to creep into his hair, and the short, well-trimmed mustache and goatee showed lighter hues as well.

Bolan knew that the pressure of running any huge business—legal or otherwise—got to a man.

McFarley extended his hand and Bolan shook it. "I've been wanting to meet you, boyo," the Irishman told Bolan with a big smile. "Ever since you started beating up my heavyweights."

It was a statement rather than a question, so Bolan remained silent.

"I'm hungry," McFarley said. "Let's eat." He turned and led Bolan to a long banquet table, much as Sugar had done earlier on the way to the elevator. But, Bolan noted, the view following McFarley wasn't nearly as interesting as it had been when he'd trailed the woman in the see-through shift.

Places had been set at the head of the table, and just to the left-hand side. Bolan couldn't help but wonder if McFarley was trying to send him a message by the seating arrangement. If so, that message had to be *I'm about to offer you an important opportunity. But you aren't my right-hand man. At least not yet.*

Bolan took his seat as a woman dressed in a low-cut French maid's outfit—nearly as sexy as Sugar's shift—brought out a bottle of white wine and two glasses. The soldier held up his hand when she started to fill his glass. "No, thanks," he said. "Just some water or iced tea, if you would."

"You don't drink?" McFarley said in a surprised tone.

"Gave it up years ago," Bolan said. "Impaired my judgment. Almost got me killed a time or two."

"Smart, boyo," the Irishman said. "I drink. But lightly."

He chuckled as he turned toward the French maid. "Too much alcohol interferes with my true pleasures in life. Just half a glass, Maria," he said, running his hand up under the back of the woman's short skirt as she poured his wine.

A moment later, the woman he had called Maria left the room and returned with salads for the two men. Another quick trip through a swing door brought a variety of salad dressings in silver bowls. Both times, she gave Bolan a lewd smile like the one he'd gotten from Sugar downstairs. She also exaggerated her bend when she set the bowls on the table, allowing her already short black skirt to ride up over her bare buttocks.

There were a lot of different crimes that were coordinated in this house, the soldier realized. But if there was one theme that ran through all of the operations it was sex. Bolan was a warrior, not a psychologist. But it didn't take a Freud or Jung to see that McFarley had an enormous appetite—or more likely an addiction—to amorous adventures with the opposite gender.

McFarley began to eat and Bolan followed suit. The kitchen was obviously on the other side of the swing door—unusual here on the fifth story of the mansion. It appeared that, like the installation of the elevator, McFarley had done some extensive remodeling within the old house.

When the salads were finished, Maria appeared holding a silver tray. The smell of roast duck wafted through the room as she set it down, this time doing so on the other side of the table from Bolan to allow him a view of the cleavage barely hidden by her low-scooped, laced neckline. Several more trips brought out bowls of potatoes and vegetables. As well as more exposures of female flesh.

"Not a bad spread," Bolan said, breaking the silence.

"You talking about the food or the waitress, Mr. Cooper?" McFarley laughed.

"I meant the food," Bolan said. "But the scenery isn't bad, either."

"Nothing but the best around here," McFarley replied. "Sure beats a po'boy on Bourbon Street. Or the disease-ridden hookers who work the jazz clubs."

"It does indeed," Bolan said.

McFarley laughed out loud. "Our waitress also works downstairs," he said. "She's yours later, Mr. Cooper, if you'd like. And it's on the house. Any of the girls you want. And however many you can handle—if you're into that sort of thing."

Bolan nodded. "If you're giving me gifts like that, you'd better start calling me Matt. Mr. Cooper just doesn't quite have the right ring for an orgy."

"All right then, Matt, me boyo," McFarley said in a thick brogue. "And while I don't extend this to many of my other employees, I think you should call me Tommy."

"You sure you want to do that?" Bolan asked as Maria sliced a large piece of duck breast and set it on his plate. "I'm just a gym manager."

McFarley laughed again. "Not after tonight," he said. "I've got a feeling about you, Matt Cooper." He paused for a second then went on. "Plus, I know far more about your past than you think I do," he said in a slightly lower voice.

I doubt that, Bolan thought. The fact was he knew exactly what the man knew about him. Aware that McFarley had connections high within the New Orleans Police Department, Bolan had seen to it that Aaron "the Bear" Kurtzman, Stony Man Farm's wheelchair-bound computer expert, had hacked into police files the world over and set up dummy files for Matt Cooper. They included arrests in many of the same criminal activities McFarley engaged in.

But no convictions.

The types, and vast number of arrests, had told McFarley that Matt Cooper was a player.

The lack of convictions told him that Cooper was smart.

"My question is," McFarley asked after swallowing a mouthful of roast duck, "why did you want a job as a gym manager in the first place? It's like a neurosurgeon working in a car wash."

"Without boring you with the details," Bolan said, "I presently find it advantageous to keep a low profile. There's been a misunderstanding between two parties I worked with. It'll blow over with time, but right now, I need something that keeps me out of the limelight within our own peculiar little loops."

The Irishman scooped up a forkful of green peas and stuck the utensil in his mouth as he nodded. When he had swallowed again, he said, "I understand." He started to cut another piece of duck with his knife and fork, then stopped. "You know, Matt," he said, "with your experience you might be more valuable to me in other areas besides managing my gym."

Bolan reached for a bowl of applesauce and spooned some onto his plate. "I've already told you, Tommy," he said, finally using the man's first name. "I'm laying low for a while."

"When you're with me," McFarley said, "you've got nothing to worry about. We can change your name if it'd make you feel better. Even change your face if you'd like. I've got a cosmetic surgeon who—"

"That's okay," Bolan interrupted. "I've had my face changed a couple of times in the past. That's enough."

The statement was *not* an idle comment. It was the truth.

"Good enough, then, laddie," McFarley said. "I don't think you'll be running across any of the people you've worked with in the past anyway. I've got my own pipelines, and like you said, we've got 'loops' not just one 'loop.' We may know what the other folk who do our kind of business are doing, but we aren't in league with them all."

Maria returned, clearing the table of dishes and bowls, and

making sure Bolan got a good look at her again, both top and bottom.

"Are you up for dessert?" McFarley asked.

"I'm already stuffed," Bolan said. "Better skip it. Besides, who knows which of your boxers I'm going to have to beat up tomorrow?"

McFarley stood up. "Like I told you," he said. "Your days at the gym are over. I can hire any number of punch-drunk old fighters to hold the heavy bag and mop the floor of that place. The only time you need to go back there is to get whatever clothes and other things you moved into that pathetic little bedroom behind the office." He stopped talking for a moment, then said, "Let's adjourn to my office."

Bolan followed the Irishman out of the room, down another hallway in what he had already seen was a labyrinth— almost a maze—of short halls and rooms. The entire top floor of the mansion had obviously been gutted, then redesigned to fit McFarley's tastes. It was nothing if not confusing, and Bolan couldn't help but suspect the man had set it up that way in case the unlikely police raid ever occurred. Without a map of the floor, it would take officers looking for drugs, illegal weapons, or any other evidence of crime extra seconds, if not minutes, to search the entire floor.

Seconds and minutes in which evidence could be destroyed. Or be used to effect an escape.

The Executioner reminded himself to spend as much time up here as he could in order to get the layout into his head. The time would come when he, probably alone, would have to search the penthouse for McFarley.

The Irishman led Bolan through a reception area, then past a desk on which several green potted plants sat. The desk also had several framed photos of what looked like family members. Bolan guessed that the older woman in some of the pictures had to be McFarley's secretary, and that the Irishman had hired her in at least some effort to separate business from pleasure. All in all, however, the reception area looked vastly out of place in what was basically a whorehouse.

Reaching into his pocket, McFarley pulled out a key and unlocked the door to his office, ushering Bolan in before flipping the light switch. The Executioner stood to the side to allow McFarley to enter, and waited while the man circled the desk to his chair.

"Have a seat wherever you'd like, Matt," the Irishman said before sitting down himself.

Bolan turned. The first thing his eyes fell upon were the wet blood stains and caking brain matter on the couch and wall behind it. "Looks like you had a hard day," he said casually, then turned toward a stuffed armchair against the side wall. "Think I'll sit over here." He walked to the chair and dropped into it. "I have this policy against intentionally sitting in freshly spilled brain matter."

Bolan had been watching McFarley out of the corner of his eye, and the expression on the man's face told him the criminal kingpin had purposely brought Matt Cooper to this office so he'd see the bloody mess. The Irishman wanted to see how he reacted. And he wanted to know if Cooper would ask about it.

Bolan didn't give him the pleasure. As soon as he'd finished his last comment, he remained silent.

Finally, McFarley broke the silence himself. "It wasn't me who had the hard day," he said. "Just one of my employees. I'm afraid he'll no longer be able to carry out his duties, Matt, and it's his job that I'm thinking about giving you." He paused to draw in a breath, his eyes still studying Bolan but getting nothing but a poker face in return. "But I want to shift the responsibilities around a little first," he finally said. "You're far more capable, I think, than he was. So you're going to have more responsibilities."

Bolan finally let his eyes return to the gore across the

room. "Well," he said, chuckling, "let's just hope I carry them out better than my predecessor."

McFarley, obviously disappointed that he hadn't gotten a reaction of fear from his new employee, became more direct. "He didn't take care of business," he said. "And he paid the price."

"Don't worry," Bolan said. "I've faced danger before a time or two."

"According to what I learned about you, it was more than a time or two."

Bolan nodded. "That was an understatement," he said. "But as I said, don't worry. Whatever the job entails, I'll get it done for you."

"Then let's quit playing footsies and get down to business," McFarley said. "As of now, you're no longer managing the gym. Let's talk about what I want you to do first. What I want you to do tomorrow, in fact."

McFarley then laid out, in detail, what Cooper would be doing the next day.

And while it hardly shocked the Executioner, he was slightly surprised. He had expected to be assigned to some form of smuggling operation—guns, drugs, or other contraband. But the act McFarley gave him was different, and Bolan recognized it for just what it was.

A test. McFarley had opened his home, his office and the girls of his brothel to the Executioner, and the Irishman had smiled and laughed throughout the entire evening as if he and Bolan had been lifelong friends. But as the criminal kingpin spoke the final few words of their multifaceted conversation that evening, Bolan could see in the man's emerald-green eyes that McFarley still didn't fully trust him.

And he'd go no farther with him until he did.

"Do you have your own weapons or do I need to furnish them for you?" McFarley asked.

"I'll be fine on my own," Bolan said.

"I understand my men took an enormous folding knife from you before."

"They did," he said. "And I'd like it back before I leave." He stood up, then suddenly reached down the front of his slacks and brought out the North American Arms Pug. Setting it silently on McFarley's desk, he said, "But they completely missed this."

The Executioner sat back down in the stuffed armchair.

McFarley's bright green eyes stared furiously at the tiny handgun on his desk. It was a good minute before he finally spoke again. When he did, he said, "I'd say you are to be congratulated on breaching my security, Matt. Very skillfully done. And it took balls." The laugh he gave out now was forced. "No pun intended." Reaching out, he lifted the NAA in his hand, looked at it, then tossed it back over his desk.

Bolan caught the little gun in midair.

"Take it," McFarley said. "If you'd planned on using it on me, you'd have already done it."

The Executioner nodded and dropped the Pug into the side pocket of his sport coat.

"But while you're to be congratulated, my men are going to have to be disciplined," McFarley said.

"I wouldn't be too hard on them," Bolan said. "It's not fair to compare them to me."

Then McFarley returned to his genuine laughter. "You don't lack confidence, do you, boyo?"

"If you don't believe in yourself," Bolan said, "how can you expect anyone else to believe in you?"

"I can't argue with that logic," McFarley said. He stood up behind his desk, indicating that the meeting was over. "My chauffeur will take you back to the gym to get your things. I own an apartment and condominium development a few miles from here, and he'll help you get settled into one of the units.

"What I told you I wanted done, I want done tomorrow.

But I'm not much of a morning person. Shall we meet here for lunch before you go off to complete your work?"

"Lunch sounds fine," Bolan said, standing up and shaking McFarley's hand.

"But wait, I almost forgot," the criminal kingpin said. "I offered you the ladies. Want a few hours down below with Maria or some of the other girls?"

"Sometime, but not tonight. I've got a move to make and a plan to develop so I can get your job done tomorrow and stay out of jail after I've done it."

McFarley nodded. "You're a man of great self-control," he said. "I like that."

"I like it, too," Bolan said.

A moment later he was being led through the hallways by O'Banion and Westbrook, descending in the elevator and being walked to the front door of the brothel. When the shorter of the men opened the door for him, Bolan stopped and held out his hand.

"What is it you want?" the short man asked.

"My knife," Bolan said.

The shorter man smiled. "I was thinking I'd just keep it myself," he said. "Got to playing with it when you were having dinner. I like it."

"I like it, too," Bolan said as he reached into the side pocket of his sport coat, brought out the NAA .22 Magnum revolver and shoved it under the goon's nose. "That's why I want it back."

"Where'd *that* come from?" the short man asked, looking cross-eyed down at the barrel.

"I brought it in with me," Bolan said as he cocked the tiny firearm. "You missed it. Now give me the knife."

Slowly, the man with the gun in his face reached into his own jacket and pulled out the Cold Steel folding knife.

Bolan clipped the weapon to his belt over his right hip, then pocketed the Pug again.

He waited while the chauffeur opened the limo door for him, then slid into the backseat of the vehicle.

5

Whenever a police officer was murdered, all cops around the world, both the dirty and the clean, took it personally. And they dropped whatever else they were doing to find the killer responsible.

Unless, of course, they were in on the murder themselves.

Bolan knew that while New Orleans had a reputation for police and politicians "on the take," there were still far more honest cops in the Big Easy than crooked men and women in blue.

But what McFarley wanted him to do was a little more complicated. The big boss of the Big Easy wanted him to kill a cop who had been on the take, then had a sudden change of heart and had become irritatingly honest.

McFarley's closing words of the night before still hung in the Executioner's ears: "This SOB—Greg Kunkle's his name—went to some church revival or something and got reborn. Now he not only won't take the payoffs I was getting to him, he's busted one of my smaller brothels and popped two of my crack dealers down in the French Quarter. I want him dead."

Bolan had placed his suitcases and equipment bags on the bed in the luxury one-bedroom apartment to which McFarley's chauffeur had driven him after a quick stop at the gym. In the wee small hours of the dark New Orleans night, he unzipped a short nylon case and opened the same locked hard plastic box he'd looked at earlier in the evening when deciding on what weaponry to take to the meeting with McFarley.

He was no longer posing as a boxing gym manager. The fake police records Kurtzman had set up for him had obviously made McFarley trust him enough to talk more openly. But this hit on NOPD Detective Greg Kunkle was a clear test of loyalty, as well as a way for McFarley to get leverage over Cooper.

Knowledge of a professional execution would be a big hammer that McFarley could hold over his head from then on. A few hints to the right ears, done the right way, could point the finger at Bolan as triggerman without involving McFarley himself.

But Bolan had different plans, and as he looked inside his pistol case, he realized there was no longer any reason not to go fully armed from here on.

The soldier removed his sport coat and slid into the black leather and nylon shoulder rig that housed the Beretta 93-R under his left arm. The rig was custom built to accommodate the sound suppressor threaded onto the extended barrel, and while the term "silencer" was one most often used by the combat noninitiated, the device did keep the noise down to a bare minimum and changed the sound to one less like a gunshot.

Bolan attached the retainer strap beneath the holster to his belt, securing it into place. Then his hands moved to his other side. Held in place by a pair of Concealex plastic magazine carriers were two extra 9 mm mags. While the Beretta itself was filled with RBCD total fragmentation rounds, one of the magazines in the front had been loaded with Hornady hollowpoints. They would pierce slightly deeper than the

RBCDs, but still mushroom into an impressive mushroom-head-looking missile that rivaled a .45 in size.

The third magazine in the Concealex holder was filled with needle-pointed armor-piercing rounds. They were made for penetration in case the target took refuge behind metal or some other hard object, or was wearing a bullet-resistant vest.

Bolan double-checked to make sure the Cold Steel Espada was clipped to the back of his belt. Satisfied that the gigantic folding knife was in place, he unbuckled his belt and slid the Concealex holster onto the rear slot, stopping it just in front of the second belt loop of his pants. Then, threading it on through the second slot, he slipped it through the last belt loop and buckled it again. A second later, the Desert Eagle had been pushed down inside the plastic holder, making a clicking sound. A clip-on double magazine carrier, which was big enough to accommodate two more of the Israeli-made .44 Magnum box-magazines came next, and Bolan clipped it just behind his left kidney.

The Espada was flanked by the Desert Eagle and its spare rounds.

But there was one extremely important weapon that Bolan wanted with him again, and he reached into the side pocket of his jacket where he'd placed it while still at McFarley's. The .22 Magnum Pug had passed through McFarley's security earlier. But this time he wanted it as a backup piece for his .44 Magnum and 9 mm Parabellum rounds. Inserting it into a tiny leather inside-the-waistband holster, he clipped it over his belt, positioning it against his back and using the spare magazine holder that sported his extra Desert Eagle ammo to wedge it into place. When he was searched again—and he suspected he would be—McFarley's man would take the Desert Eagle but likely leave the magazines in place.

At least the Executioner hoped he would. After all, the magazines would be no good without the pistol to go with them.

There was only one problem with the Pug as he saw it; he

had not had time to test fire it. And Bolan never trusted *any* weapon he hadn't personally fired.

The soldier sat down on the edge of the bed. An hour ago, had someone asked him if there was any sort of combat or criminal problem he'd never faced before, his answer would have been none that he could think of.

But finally he had thought of one. Or, rather, McFarley had thought one up for him.

Bolan lay back on the bed and rested on his elbow. His policy was to never kill cops—clean or dirty. He had in the past made an occasional exception.

And to make matters more complicated in this case, according to McFarley, Kunkle had repented of his past sins and was doing his best to make amends. He was no longer even dirty. He was a new man, different from the one who'd worked both sides of the law in the past.

So Bolan was going to have to fake the hit, convince McFarley that he'd killed Kunkle without actually doing so.

The Executioner had faked similar hits in the past, with the intended victims' willing to help—and they were almost always willing because they knew if they didn't help put their enemy in jail he'd just hire someone else to kill them. Bolan had taken photos of ketchup-covered bodies and used other props to make the death look real.

But this job was to be different. McFarley was familiar with the way cops posing undercover as hit men faked murders, and he wanted more solid proof.

McFarley wanted Greg Kunkle's *hands*. With his police connections, McFarley could get the fingerprints run through AFIS—the nation-wide Advanced Fingerprint Identification System—and since all law-enforcement personnel were printed when hired, he could see if the prints on file matched the prints on the severed hands.

Which made the operation a hundred times more complicated.

An idea had been floating around in the back of Bolan's mind for some time, and suddenly it crystallized. Pulling the cell phone from his shirt pocket, he tapped in Barbara Price's number at Stony Man Farm.

As he'd known she would, Price answered.

"I need some help," Bolan said without preamble. "Can you transfer me to the Bear?"

"You're on your way now. I'll scramble the call," Price said.

A moment later, Kurtzman answered with, "Hello, Striker. Always nice to hear your voice and know you're still alive."

"You pays your money and you takes your chances." Bolan quoted an old saying. "But since you brought up the subject of death, let me tell you what I need from you." He began running down the elements of the McFarley-Kunkle situation to the computer expert.

"This sounds fairly simple," Kurtzman said. "Hal can ask his contacts to get hands from a donated corpse at Georgetown's medical school. Enough people owe the guy favors." He paused. "I realize the body was donated to science, surely the hands can be sacrificed to a greater good."

"As soon as you get the hands," Bolan went on, "make a set of prints and substitute them for Kunkle's on AFIS. But first, run them for real to make sure they don't pop up on their own. If the hands' former owner was ever printed—criminal record, armed forces, or for any other reason—they'll pop up double when McFarley has whatever dirty cops he uses check them. And we don't need that complicating this mess."

"Already thought of that," Kurtzman said. "If the new prints are already on file, I can delete them. Or get another pair of hands on the job . Sorry. Really bad pun, there, I realize."

"I'll let it slide," Bolan said. "But as soon as you've printed the hands, get all of the ink off and then put them on ice and send them this way with Jack Grimaldi. Tell him to fly a pontoon plane of some sort. I'll meet him in the swamp at coordinates that I'll come up with later."

"You want anyone with him?" Kurtzman asked.

Bolan knew what the computer man was thinking; he had thought of it himself. It was great to think that Kunkle had experienced such a dramatic change of heart, but he was still responsible for the laws he'd broken before. And if he was *really* sincere in his new belief, he'd know he still had to pay.

Bolan planned on sending Kunkle, blindfolded, back to the Farm to be secured during the rest of this mission by blacksuits. So it might not be a bad idea to have a couple of those blacksuits with Grimaldi in case the New Orleans cop did a little "backsliding" on the way back. When Bolan had finished with McFarley, Kunkle would be returned to New Orleans to face charges for bribery and any other crimes he'd committed while in McFarley's pocket.

Kunkle might well have experienced a genuine religious experience. But he was going to have to confess his sins to the district attorney in addition to God. If the formerly dirty cop helped them out, Bolan suspected Brognola would use his influence within the Justice Department to get Kunkle a light sentence. Maybe even a suspended one.

"Yeah," the Executioner said as soon as all of these things had run through his mind. "Send a couple of blacksuits—in plain clothes—as guards. Kunkle will be flying back with them. And staying for a while."

"Like that Motel-6-guy says, 'We'll keep a light on for him.'" Kurtzman laughed.

"Sounds good," Bolan said. "In the mean time, I've got a cop to go kidnap."

And with that, he pushed the button and ended the call.

6

Bolan rose from the bed and pulled the .22 Magnum Pug from between his back and the .44 caliber magazine caddy. He figured it had a 99% chance of working properly—everything he had ever used from North American Arms had done its job the first time "out of the chute." But he would not put one-hundred percent faith in any gun he hadn't actually fired himself, so he lifted the tiny-but-powerful revolver in his hand. He could cover the entire weapon just by closing his fist around it. And folks could say what they wanted about .22 Magnum guns being "mouse guns." Bolan knew that good shot placement was far more important than caliber, and he viewed the little revolver more like two-and-a-half .44 Magnums when it came to killing power.

The Executioner stared down at the snub-nosed Pug for a moment. Then, grabbing a pillow off the bed, he took three steps to the desk on the other side of the room and found a thick New Orleans phone book in the bottom drawer. The Pug was already loaded with hollowpoint rounds, and the hammer rested on one of the safety grooves between each of the chambers. That prevented an accidental discharge should the minute revolver be struck on the hammer, or dropped.

Kneeling, Bolan placed the phone book on the floor and

doubled the pillow up on top of it. Then, cocking the hammer and jamming it tightly down into the pillow, he pulled the trigger.

The explosion sent a flurry of feathers floating into the air, and the sound was comparable to a tiny firecracker going off—not silent, but not loud enough to leave the apartment, either. When he dug down into the phone book, Bolan saw that the fragmented pieces of the bullet had gone three-quarters of the way through the pages.

The gun worked and worked well.

Sliding the loading rod out from beneath the barrel, Bolan removed the cylinder and used the same rod to knock the slightly expanded brass casing from the wheel. He replaced it with a live round, then reassembled the weapon and lowered the hammer onto another of the safety notches. Satisfied that the 5-round minirevolver would serve him well—at least within the limitations of its design—Bolan replaced the Pug against his back.

The Beretta 93-R machine pistol. The Desert Eagle .44 Magnum power blaster. The Cold Steel Espada, and the North American Arms .22 Magnum Pug. These were the four weapons on which Bolan would rely because each served a very different purpose. He always worked on the assumption that you were never over-armed until you carried so much steel that it adversely affected your balance and movement. And he wasn't close to that point yet.

McFarley had given Bolan a picture of Kunkle, along with the fact that the born-again New Orleans detective was working the French Quarter that night. As he reclined back on the bed again, Bolan held the picture up to his eyes and stared at it. Kunkle looked to be in his late fifties, with wrinkle lines covering his forehead. The information McFarley had written on the back of the photo told Bolan that while the NOPD detective had once been known to spend his breaks in the strip clubs and bars famous for live sex shows, he had taken to frequenting the less-decadent Pat O'Brien's since his conversion to Christianity.

If a true conversion had actually taken place, Bolan thought. In any case, it was O'Brien's where Bolan intended to find him.

Or, more accurately, kidnap him.

Bolan glanced at his wristwatch. It was nearly midnight. Late for most people.

But Bourbon Street would be in full swing.

Fully armed, the Executioner left the apartment and hailed a cab near the entrance to the apartment complex. A few moments later, he was in the back seat and heading for New Orleans' world-famous French Quarter.

BOURBON STREET, IN THE MIDDLE of the famous French Quarter, had been called the Amsterdam of America. And for good reason. For a straight seven street blocks, it was difficult to tell the difference between weeknights and weekends. And had it not been for the sun rising and setting, the difference between 7:00 a.m. and midnight would have been negligible as well. The area featured bars, souvenir shops, strip clubs, restaurants and jazz clubs. The party never ended until the patrons, individually, decided it was time to go home. Or passed out on the floor. And there was a constant string of newcomers always ready to take their place.

Like most of New Orleans, the French Quarter had been hit by Hurricane Katrina and, here and there, there was still evidence of the mighty storm's destruction. But as the prime moneymaker as well as the most famous landmark of the city, it had been among the first areas to be rebuilt after the devastation.

The sounds, sights and smells of Bourbon Street infiltrated Bolan's senses as he paid the cabdriver and got out. From one side of the street, he could hear the booming music of Guns n' Roses. From the other came the music of AC/DC, and from farther down the street chords of a Lynyrd Skynrd song threatened to overtake all the other bands. The sidewalks and streets were packed with tourists and local, stumbling drunks. Many carried plastic cups filled with alcoholic beverages not finished when they'd decided to leave the last place on their "pub crawling" route.

Jimmy Buffett's "It's Five O'Clock Somewhere" blasted in Bolan's ears as he stepped onto the sidewalk and began making his way toward Pat O'Brien's. He passed various restaurants and bars—the Famous Door, Razzoo and the Krazy Corner—and was tempted to cover his ears as more music exploded as loud as any gunfire. Glancing upward over a sign announcing the Cats Meow nightclub, Bolan saw an attractive and abundantly built blonde girl look down at him, grin, then lift the tail of her T-shirt to her neck, exposing a pair of enormous breasts.

Bolan was only human. He smiled back at her as he moved on.

He continued to walk carefully, dodging the inebriated, off-balance pedestrians on the sidewalk with the skill of a running back hitting open field. Finally, he saw the sign he was looking for in the distance: Pat O'Brien's.

The club was actually divided into three parts with different atmospheres of rowdiness, and was the home of the world-famous Hurricane, a red rum concoction that came served in large souvenir glasses. Men and women poured in and out of the doors, some returning their glasses for a three-dollar refund as they left.

According to McFarley, Kunkle had chosen the least rambunctious area of Pat O'Brien's as his hangout of choice since his conversion. So it was to the piano-bar section of the building that Bolan now headed. He spotted the man from his picture, alone at a table, almost immediately. Kunkle had medium-long, light brown hair that fell halfway over his ears and draped long over his collar in the back. His full beard—

the same light brown as his hair—made him look like he'd stepped off the set of some seventies cop movie. He wore a light summer tweed sport coat, a white shirt and a tie loosened at the neck. The soldier was close enough to hear him order a Diet Coke from the waiter who had just appeared.

"Make that two," Bolan told the waiter as the man turned away.

The waiter just nodded and hurried off again.

The dual pianos in the bar continued to play as Bolan, not bothering to ask first, took a seat at the table across from Kunkle. The New Orleans police detective looked at Bolan with a blank face.

"I've been expecting this," he said quietly without the slightest trace of surprise in his voice.

Bolan nodded. Kunkle had known that McFarley would send someone to kill him when he'd turned against the criminal kingpin. And he thought that time had come. What he didn't realize was that while that was exactly why the Executioner had been sent to O'Brien's, Bolan had no intention of carrying out McFarley's order.

But Kunkle didn't need to know that. At least not yet. It looked to Bolan as if the man had accepted his fate, which meant he might be able to get the detective out of the French Quarter more quietly if the man didn't know the rest of the story.

As he settled into his chair, Bolan reached behind his back. Closing a big fist around the .22 Magnum Pug, he kept it covered until his hand had disappeared beneath the table. Then, silently waiting for a lull in the music coming from the pianos, he cocked the mini revolver.

Kunkle heard the metallic sound and recognized it for what it was.

"Take a look under the table to make sure," Bolan whispered.

Kunkle slid slightly back in his chair, then dipped an eye below the tabletop. Sitting back up, he said, "It's a little one."

"But it'll do the trick," Bolan replied.

Kunkle's face still showed no surprise or concern, and the soldier knew the man believed he was just what he was posing as—an assassin sent by McFarley to exact retribution for Kunkle's change of heart.

"You going to do it right here?" the detective asked quietly.

"Not unless you make me," Bolan said just as quietly. "In fact, if you cooperate, I'm not going to do it at all."

The first show of any emotion crinkled the eyebrows of the formerly corrupt cop. "You'll have to excuse me if I'm a little confused," he said.

"All you need to know is that this isn't quite what you think it is," Bolan said. "And that if we get along, and things go like I want them to, you're not going to die. At least right now. Or by my hand."

The words brought a soft, ironic snort from the man seated across the table. "I accept Christ as my personal savior, quit ignoring Tommy McFarley's illegal operations, quit taking his payoffs, and a man aims a gun at me under the table and cocks it." He paused and the snort turned into an ironic chuckle. "And I'm not supposed to think he's here to kill me? You'll excuse me if I have a hard time believing that. I know what I've done, and I deserve to pay for it."

Beneath the table, Bolan lowered the .22 Magnum revolver's hammer and rolled the cylinder to one of the safety notches. Then his fingers closed around the weapon to hide it from curious eyes as he returned it behind his back. "Stand up and come with me," he ordered. "You've got my word that you're going to come out of all this a lot better than you think right now."

Kunkle had accepted his fate and he did as told. He stood up. When Bolan motioned for him to lead the way toward the door, he did that, too.

They never did get their Diet Cokes.

A few seconds later, they were back on Bourbon Street, amid the music and yelling voices, looking for another cab.

DAWN HAD BROKEN BY THE TIME Bolan and Kunkle reached the parking lot of the Cajun Creek Tour Company, ten miles south of New Orleans, on the Mississippi Delta peninsula. A lone man with long shaggy gray hair and a matching beard had parked a broken-down Chevy pickup in the otherwise deserted parking lot. As they pulled up in front of him, they saw him fumbling with a huge key ring in front of the door to the seedy-looking office.

Beyond the office, in the muddy water of the swampy shore, a dozen or so airboats of varying sizes were docked and ready for the tourist trade.

Bolan paid the cabbie, and he and Kunkle got out of the backseat. In addition to his other armament, the soldier also carried Kunkle's SIG-Sauer 9 mm pistol and the man's backup gun, a small NAA .380. Manufactured by the same firm that produced Bolan's minirevolver, the .380 was smaller than most .25s or .22s on the market. Bolan had also noticed that it was equipped with a Crimson Trace laser grip. With the push of a button—which came naturally when grasping the little weapon—a bright red spot was projected on the target rendering the use of the sights unnecessary. Kunkle had willingly turned both guns over to Bolan right after they'd entered the cab.

"My mama used to tell me I'd end up as some alligator's dinner," the New Orleans detective said as they started toward the small office building. "I've always heard they take you under and drown you, then wait a day or so in order to sort of 'tenderize' you. Guess I'm about to find out."

The two men were still out of earshot of the man opening the office door, and Bolan whispered, "That's not going to happen. Not if you do everything I tell you to." He studied the man closely out of the corner of his eye.

It was too early to tell, and Kunkle had not been tested in his newfound faith. But so far, he had struck Bolan as sincere in his conversion to Christianity and his decision to turn back into an honest cop. Bolan would keep an eye on the man until he could be sure, but his instincts told him that Kunkle was a good man gone astray. He was the perfect "prodigal son." He had been lured, little by little, into a world of decadence and payoffs. But it appeared that the revival he had attended had hit him hard, and the Executioner's gut feelings had rarely failed him in the past. If it turned out that Kunkle was indeed repentant, Bolan knew he could use someone to watch his back during this mission. If he was going to use Kunkle in that role, however, he needed to test the man's conversion soon.

So, as always seemed to happen at some point in any operation, he decided to take a calculated risk.

Stepping quickly in front of Kunkle as they continued to descend the bank toward the office, Bolan stopped the man in his tracks. Pulling the SIG-Sauer from his waistband, and the minute .380 from a pocket, he handed the guns, grip first, to the detective and whispered, "I'm trusting you to be on my side now. But you turn on me, and you'll be meeting Jesus a lot sooner than you thought." He paused as the New Orleans detective took his weapons, his face a mask of surprise. "Keep them out of sight," Bolan finished.

Kunkle still looked as if someone had just handed him a rattlesnake instead of his own guns. Slowly, with almost robotlike movements, he pulled back the tail of his sport coat and shoved the SIG back down into the holster he still wore on his strong side. The NAA .380 went into the right back pocket of his pants.

Bolan studied the man's eyes for further reaction. Kunkle had been resigned to becoming alligator chum, and had hardly spoken a word during their drive from the city. The man almost seemed to welcome what he thought was his imminent murder, as if by dying he could at least escape the humiliation of arrest and imprisonment. He had remained calm, and Bolan chalked that up to his newfound faith, and the fact that—even as dirty as he'd been—he believed he was about to go to a far better place than this world.

The two men began walking again, reaching the man at the door just as he found the right key and twisted it in the lock. He turned to look at them, then leaned to the side and spit a long stream of chewing tobacco onto the concrete. The thick brown liquid hit and exploded like a miniature bomb, splashing dangerously close to Kunkle's shoes. The gray-haired man turned toward them before pushing open the door. "We not never open for another hour," he said in a thick Cajun accent.

"You will be today," Bolan said as he reached into his pants pocket and pulled out a money clip loaded with bills. Peeling off ten hundreds, he shoved them into the man's hand. "There's another thousand waiting for you when we get back," he said in a low voice.

The man didn't hesitate. He grabbed the proffered money and jammed it into one of the chest pockets of his dirty, fish-smelling denim overalls. "You know exactly where you want to go?" he asked.

Bolan reached into his other pocket and pulled out a handheld Ground Positioning System. "Exactly," he said.

"Then let's be go," the man in the faded denim overalls said. "And don't you be tellin' me no more. Don't want to know what we about to do. Don't care. I just drive the airboat."

Bolan nodded. He suspected the man believed they were about to make a drug pickup of some sort, which was fine. The less the boatman knew the better.

Bolan and Kunkle followed the man down a set of cracked

concrete steps to an airboat. On the way down, Kunkle lagged back slightly, then whispered into the Executioner's ear. "Please," he said. "I deserve it. But not this guy, okay?"

Bolan turned toward the detective and saw the worry lines covering his face. "I don't intend to hurt him," he whispered back as they caught up to the boatman at the bow of his airboat. "And as for you, do you really think I'd have given you your guns back if I was going to kill you?"

Kunkle stared at Bolan, his eyes full of confusion. He could tell the detective didn't understand about the guns being returned. From where he stood, it was a complete contradiction, and none of what they were doing made any sense to him.

"We take this one for sure," the Cajun said as they reached the dock. "Got's it a 454 Chevy Engine and it go up to thirty-five mile an hour. Go anywhere there an inch of water, too. Any place you want go in the swamp." He stepped off the pier onto the deck. "But somehow, I no get the feelin' you boys here to see gators."

"No, we're not," Bolan said.

"Well, that okay," the boatman said as he untied the line from the dock cleat. "This time a year, we see plenty gator whether you want or not."

Bolan and Kunkle boarded the airboat and took seats in the first row of the six passenger stadium chairs bolted to the deck. The boatman revved up the powerful Chevy engine, and a moment later they were blasting air back toward the shore.

"You gimme that GP-thing," the boatman said, extending a hand behind him as he manned the wheel with the other. "I get you there to get whatever you gettin'."

Bolan handed him the GPS.

"This tim'a year," the Cajun said, "water not so high. Not so many shortcuts." He stopped speaking, reached into another chest pocket of his overalls and produced a small half-pint bottle of some kind of clear liquid. Taking a long swig, he held it behind him. "You boys want drink?" he asked. "Got plenty. Best stuff your tongue ever wrap around. Made by my Uncle Pierre."

"It's a little early for me," Bolan said.

"I'd better pass, too," Kunkle replied.

The fumes of whatever sort of moonshine was in the bottle drifted back to the men in the chairs. "Whatever it is," Kunkle whispered to Bolan, "it's strong enough to give you a contact high."

The Cajun boatman heard him and laughed. He increased the speed of the boat, weaving in and out of the marshy swampland as if he'd done it every day of his life. And Bolan suspected that wasn't much of an exaggeration. Here and there, the hungry eyes of alligators appeared above the water and, like a man driving a car and trying to avoid dogs, the boatman swerved this way, then that.

"You boys want a gator long as you here?" the Cajun asked. "Good eatin', them."

"Just get us to the coordinates on the GPS," Bolan said. "Then, when we get back, you'll get your other thousand."

"Fair enough for me," the man said, shrugging at the wheel of the airboat.

Fifteen minutes later, after they had skimmed across the water at breakneck speed, the Cajun let up on the gas and let the boat drift in the water.

Thirty yards away—just outside the swampland and in the Gulf of Mexico proper—Bolan could see the pontoon plane floating. Squinting, he could even see Jack Grimaldi—Stony man Farm's number one pilot—through the glass, behind the controls.

"I be guessin' this be the place," the boatman said. "Want me to float 'er on out to the plane?"

Bolan just nodded.

Thirty seconds later, they came alongside the pontoon

plane. The passenger's door opened, and a man Bolan had never seen before—undoubtedly one of the blacksuit trainees from the Farm as he'd requested—extended a small plastic ice chest.

Bolan took it, then set it on one of the unoccupied chairs next to him.

"Hello, Sarge," Grimaldi said from inside the plane.

Bolan could barely see his old friend, but he nodded anyway, and said, "Good morning, Jack." Turning back to the chest, Bolan blocked the boatman's view with his body, then quickly opened the lid of the ice chest . Frozen beneath a thin layer of ice cubes, and on top of even more ice, Bolan could see a pair of severed men's hands.

Grimaldi leaned over the blacksuit as Bolan closed the lid. "That what you needed?" he asked.

"That's it. I assume the Bear ran them and they were clean."

"Clean as a hound's tooth," Grimaldi said. "An expression I've never quite understood, since I've never seen a dog yet who brushes his teeth or flosses."

The blacksuit spoke again, his eyes on Kunkle. "This the man we're to take back?" he asked.

Bolan hesitated a moment. That had been his original plan—the one he'd run by Kurtzman. They could blindfold Kunkle, and keep him sightless until he was secured and under guard in one of Stony Man Farm's main house bedrooms. But the soldier's gut now told him that what he'd thought of earlier—having Kunkle to watch his back—might be a better approach to the next phases of this mission.

Should he alter his battle strategy and keep Kunkle with him? The man certainly knew New Orleans, and the bayous around it, better than he did.

The question was, could Kunkle really be trusted? Many a criminal had tried to pull what was known in law-enforcement circles as the Christian Hustle. They pretended to have had a spiritual awakening when all they were really doing was attempting to get a lighter sentence or impress their parole board.

Then again, there were the rare times when the bad guys really *did* experience a conversion and a change of heart.

And Bolan's instincts told him that Kunkle was one of those rare birds who was sincere. But he would have to extend his trust for the man little by little, just to make sure.

Finally, Bolan answered. "This *was* the guy," he told the blacksuit, "but I've changed my mind. I'm going to keep him with me a little longer. He can be of more use down here than he can be locked away."

The blacksuit shrugged.

Grimaldi—whose head was still visible as he leaned across the plane—said, "Whatever you think, big guy. As always, it's your call."

The Executioner turned toward Kunkle. The man looked even more confused than he already had been.

"He stays with me," Bolan said. "Take care, Jack." He motioned to the boatman to turn the airboat around and take them back, and saw a deep frown of confusion on the Cajun's face, as well.

Bolan knew where the expression came from. The Cajun had watched Bolan take possession of a container that he would just naturally believe held drugs or some other kind of contraband. But he had not seen any money change hands. Of course, Bolan knew, some drug deals were done in two places at the same time with the money being kept separate to hold down evidence should there be a bust. But that usually entailed at least a cell phone call during the simultaneous procedure to make sure each party was holding up its end. And there had been no such communication here.

In any case, they were soon speeding back into the swampland and the pontoon plane could be heard taking off behind them.

"Don't know what you got in that box," the boatman said above the sound of the wind. "And don't want to know. I take you on back now, and you give me more money, right?"

Bolan wasn't so sure the man was being truthful when he said he didn't care what was in the cooler. He had picked up on a shifty, nervous feeling that emanated from the boatman. But he played along with the game anyway, and he decided he might as well use the drug smuggler cover to its fullest. "That's the plan," Bolan said. "And you keep your mouth shut about ever even seeing us. You'll stay a lot healthier if you never saw us."

"See who?" the Cajun said. "I don't see nobody so far today. He glanced at the wristwatch on his arm. "Fact a' matter be, I still not even open for business."

Fifteen minutes later, they pulled back into one of the slips at the dock and the Cajun boatman tied them off to the same cleat. Bolan and Kunkle stepped up onto the dock with the Executioner carrying the ice chest by the handles on the ends.

Kunkle continued to look confused. But as soon as they were alone again, Bolan planned to tell him the rest of the story. And then they would see just how sincere Kunkle's sudden conversion to Christianity really was.

Bolan and Kunkle started up the steps from the dock toward where they were parked. The Cajun fell a step or two behind on the narrow walkway. Bolan glanced around. There was still no one around this early in the morning, and what came next he suddenly realized he had half-expected.

"Stop your walking now and turn around," the boatman said from behind them.

The Executioner and the New Orleans detective stopped in their tracks, turning slowly toward the water. There, three steps down and just out of reach, stood the airboat man, aiming an old, blue-worn Smith & Wesson Model 10 .38 at them. He grinned, showing two rows of yellow-brown teeth.

"I thinking now you owe me more money even," the boat-man said.

Bolan looked at him. "I agreed to pay you the other half," he said. "You don't need the gun to get it."

"You got wrong-thinkin' there," the boatman said. "I thinkin' I like a take all the money you got. And the dope inside that cool box. My brother-in-law, he sell it for nice profit."

Bolan saw Kunkle out of the corner of his eye. The man didn't look afraid. And, since he was suddenly dealing with a situation he was familiar with, it had temporarily taken his mind off the confusion of what they were doing. Then, he even spoke. "And what do you plan to do with us?" he asked.

"My cousin got alligator farm not far away," the Cajun an-swered, giving an even bigger and more spectacular show of his lack of dental work. "You make nice dinner for a gator or two."

"You want our money, it's yours," Bolan said. Pulling the lapel of his jacket out slightly with his left hand, he moved his right across his body as if about to reach into an interior pocket.

"Careful," the Cajun said.

Bolan didn't speed up until his hand had passed the hidden pocket and clasped the butt of the Beretta 93-R in his shoul-der rig. Then, suddenly, so fast that the eye couldn't follow it, the same hand snapped back out and pointed the sound suppressor on the end of the weapon at the Cajun boatman's head. He had no need to use the sights, and he snapped off a pair of lightning quick 9 mm rounds, both of which both struck the Cajun just above the nose.

A split second later, Bolan heard the boom of Kunkle's SIG-Sauer and another round hit the boatman in the chest. The two subsonic and third ear-numbing round took the boat-man to the ground, the S&W .38 falling to his side.

"We'd better get out of here," Kunkle said.

Bolan nodded in agreement.

But before he could, more explosions sounded from behind them, and bullets began flying past their heads and arms.

7

The Executioner whirled as the Cajun in the overalls hit the wooden dock on his back. Dropping to one knee, he saw a white Oldsmobile sedan, which had skidded to a halt roughly twenty yards away. Two men—both vaguely familiar in his hundredth-of-a-second glance—had begun firing through the window before the vehicle had even stopped. Once it stopped, they dived from the Olds, both holding 9 mm Uzi submachine guns.

The area provided no cover or concealment, and the gunfight became simply a matter of time—who shot accurately first. The words of Wyatt Earp—Old West peace officer, frontiersman and gunfighter—flew through Bolan's head.

"Take your time…in a hurry."

Which is exactly what Bolan did.

At twenty yards, he still had no need to use the sights and he extended the hand holding the Beretta to arm's length, pointing at one of the men on the ground as if pointing with his finger. Bolan had already flipped the selector switch to 3-round-burst mode, and he pressed the trigger back and sent a trio of RBCD total fragmentation rounds toward the shooter's head. At the same time he recognized the man as Razor

Westbrook—one of McFarley's goons who had searched him at the office-brothel.

Westbrook wore a thin T-shirt under a lightweight suit in the Louisiana swamp humidity. But as soon as all three of Bolan's 9 mm rounds struck his throat, chin and nose, the suit, and undershirt, turned a dark wine color.

Next to him, the Executioner heard more explosions as Kunkle returned fire with his own weapon. Just as the other man from the Olds rolled behind the car and out of sight, Bolan's brain told him that the vague familiarity that had raced through him meant that the man was Jake Jackson— the heavyweight Bolan had knocked out in the ring and then stomped into the floor of his office the day before.

Bolan frowned as Jackson's hand extended out from beneath the car. The heavyweight fired wildly, proving that he wasn't any better as a gunfighter than he was a boxer.

The situation made no sense to Bolan. Obviously, two of McFarley's men—one of them a prizefighter who was currently hiding beneath the Olds—had tailed him and Kunkle from New Orleans' French Quarter out to the swampy marina. But why? Had the Big Easy's big boss sent them to keep an eye on Matt Cooper, the new guy? Or did they have their own, personal reasons?

Bolan didn't know, but he intended to find out. And, once again, Jackson's stupidity would afford him the chance.

Bolan fired toward the Oldsmobile, which caused the Uzi to jerk back out of sight. That was good. He wanted Jackson alive so he could find out the motive behind both the tail and the sudden attack. Turning toward the right front tire, Bolan switched the Beretta's selector switch back to semiauto and fired a lone round into the rubber.

The tire erupted into flapping rubber shrapnel as the right front side of the Oldsmobile dropped to the rim of the wheel. Another single 9 mm slug did the same to the right rear tire, and the Executioner heard a grunting sound come from under the vehicle.

Kunkle had picked up on what he had in mind and made his way around the front of the vehicle as Bolan sprinted toward the back bumper. The two men fired almost simultaneously at the front and rear tires on the driver's side of the Olds. The SIG-Sauer blasted; the Beretta quietly burped.

As the car dropped even lower, the moan beneath the chassis turned into a series of whelps that sounded more puppy-like than human. With the Oldsmobile sitting on the rims of all four wheels, Jackson was trapped between the car and the cracked concrete of the parking lot.

Bolan took his time circling the car again, stopping at the spot where he'd last seen the hand holding the Uzi. Leaning down, he could see the Israeli subgun lying uselessly on the ground. But more importantly, he could see Jackson, face up and grimacing with pain, just inside the right front flat tire.

"Get me...out of here," the boxer breathed out in painful breaths.

Bolan could see that the car was pressing firmly on the man's chest. Jackson had been forced to turn his head sideways to keep it off his face. His lips were trembling like a man who knew he was facing an imminent, slow and painful death.

Bolan leaned onto the side of the Oldsmobile, increasing the pressure on the man beneath the car. Jackson screeched again.

"Usually it's good to have a big powerful chest," Bolan said. "But right now, I'm guessing you'd rather be a skinny little featherweight."

"Please..." the man moaned. "Get me...out of here."

Bolan shifted his weight off the Olds, but left the man where he was. "Let's talk a little bit first, shall we, Jake?" he said. Then, without waiting for any more breathless words, he went on with, "Did McFarley tell you and your dead friend to follow me? Or did you come here on your own?"

"Get me...out of here...*please!*" Jackson screeched.

"Just as soon as you answer my questions," Bolan said calmly.

By this point, Kunkle had returned to Bolan's side of the car and stood next to him. "Hello, Jake," he said softly.

"Kunkle..." Jackson breathed out. "Get this...thing off...me."

"It doesn't sound like that's going to happen unless you start cooperating," Kunkle told the man.

"McFarley sent me," Jackson got out in one painful breath.

"Why?" Bolan asked.

"Because you're...new," Jake spurted. "He watches...everybody...especially since this guy's—" his eyes flickered back up to Kunkle "—betrayal." The man's face was still a mask of agony as his eyes stayed glued to the detective.

"That explains the tail," Bolan said. "Not the Uzis or the attempt to kill us." He leaned on the car lightly and this time, Jackson screamed. "Ahhh! Stop! Please!"

The Executioner let up again.

"Killing you...was my idea," he said. "You're...obviously working with Kunkle...not trying to kill him."

"And that would be a feather in your cap if you caught us together and killed us both, wouldn't it?" Bolan said. "You might even get to quit being a punching bag for better fighters and step up in the ranks to take the place of whoever's brain it was splattered all over McFarley's office."

His range of motion was limited. But Jackson nodded as best he could. "I'm...getting too old...to fight," he breathed out.

Bolan nodded, more to himself than anyone else. The question he was about to ask next was, perhaps, the most crucial of all. "Have you talked to McFarley since you spotted Kunkle and me together?" he asked.

"No," he said. "Not yet."

"Are you sure?" Bolan asked. "You spent a lot of time alone in this car with your dead friend."

"I didn't call in...I swear it," Jackson panted.

"Well, you spent a lot of time with Westbrook, following Kunkle and me out here," Bolan said again. "Then even more time waiting while we went on our boat ride." He paused and cleared his throat. "You sure you didn't make a cell phone call to McFarley to tell him what you'd found out?"

"No!" Jackson tried to shout. "I promise! I was...afraid if I did he'd...just want you to come back...so he could kill you himself."

Bolan paused a few seconds, thinking. The story might well be true. This over-the-hill club fighter might, indeed, have wanted to bring in his and Kunkle's bodies like trophies to impress the boss. And it would have been just like McFarley to prefer letting Matt Cooper believe his cover was still in place and reel him in like a fish. Before he killed Bolan, McFarley would want to find out who Cooper actually was, what law-enforcement agency he represented, how he'd manipulated his background check to look like a criminal, and exactly how much he knew about the Irishman's overall operations.

And that would have cheated Jackson out of the pleasure of killing Cooper in revenge for the humiliations he'd suffered first in the ring and then the office, the day before.

"Please!" Jackson choked out. "Please...get this thing off of me!"

Bolan glanced toward Kunkle. "I'll lift this side of the car as much as I can. You pull him out."

Kunkle nodded his understanding.

The soldier grabbed the door handle with both hands and squatted slightly, using his legs as well as his arms and shoulder to rock the Oldsmobile upward. He was unable to move the car more than an inch above Jackson's chest, but it was enough.

Kunkle pulled the man out.

Bolan set the car back down as soon as the heavyweight was clear. He looked down to see the rips, tears, and grease and oil spots covering the man's shirt. Jackson was lying on his back, coughing, still trying to catch his breath.

"Stand up," Bolan ordered.

Jackson rolled over and came up onto his hands and knees. Bolan stepped back, expecting him to rise to his feet. But then the Executioner's eyes fell on the Uzi only a few feet away.

Both Bolan and Kunkle had holstered their weapons during the "under car" interrogation. The soldier's hand shot for the butt of the Beretta in his shoulder rig as Jackson started to turn toward the Uzi. "Don't do it, Jake," the Executioner warned in a loud voice.

The heavyweight either didn't hear, didn't care, or was so bent on revenge he was willing to give up his life for it. He lunged forward and grabbed the submachine gun with both hands.

Bolan drew the Beretta. He had just enough time to say, "Don't!" one more time before Jackson turned toward him with the weapon.

The Executioner fired a lone, near-silent 9 mm round into the hump on Jackson's much-broken nose, and the heavyweight hit the "canvas" for the last time.

Bolan glanced down at his watch. People were going to start showing up around the marina any minute. They had left the Cajun dead on the dock. The other body—Razor Westbrook's—was in plain sight in the parking lot. So was Jackson's. And Bolan didn't have the time or desire to try to explain it all to the parish sheriff after someone called the carnage in.

Bending over Jackson's corpse, Bolan patted him down until he found a cell phone in the man's left hip pocket. Grabbing it, he jammed it into his waistband. "Get the cell phone off that other guy," he ordered Kunkle. "We'll dump them and see if he was telling the truth about not tipping off McFarley yet."

Kunkle turned toward Westbrook's body.

Bolan felt his eyebrows lower in concentration. They had taken a cab out here, and the Oldsmobile wasn't going far with four blown tires. His eyes turned to the ancient and battered Chevy pickup the boatman had driven. It would have to do to get them back to New Orleans.

The Executioner hurried back down the steps to where the man's lifeless form still lay. He found the big key ring he'd seen earlier and located what looked like a Chevy key among the others.

Meeting Kunkle at the pickup, Bolan slid behind the wheel and inserted the key. It took three tries, but the engine finally sputtered to life.

A moment later, Bolan and Kunkle were hightailing it away from the marina with the humid air of the swamp blowing through the open windows onto their faces.

8

"I'm trying to do as much as I can to make up for the sins I've committed," Kunkle said, bluntly breaking the silence inside the pickup as it bounced along the cracked asphalt road back toward New Orleans. "But I know that's impossible. You can't earn your way to heaven. It's a gift you either take or refuse. The good things I'm trying to do are out of gratitude for salvation, not an attempt to get it."

Bolan paused before answering. Finally, he said, "I'd like to believe you, Kunkle. And so far it looks to me like you're telling me the truth. But I've seen too many hustlers pretend to take on religion for their own selfish reasons in the past. You're just going to have to be patient. It's going to take some time before I fully trust you. And you need to know up front—even if this conversion of yours is real, you're going to have to go back to face the crimes you've committed."

Kunkle's smile looked genuine when he answered. "I know that, Mr. Cooper," he said. "And in a strange way, I welcome it. It's been a long time since I've had a clear conscience, and if it takes prison time to pay my debt, well, that's just what it'll have to be. After all, the Apostle Paul had to spend a good deal of time in prison, and if it was good enough for him, it's good enough for me."

Bolan was slightly surprised at the detective's knowledge. "It sounds like you've been spending some time with the Bible," he said.

"I have," Kunkle came back. "It's all I have left. And like I said, I'm willing to pay for my sins. But before I do, I'd really like to help you bring McFarley and his whole empire down."

Bolan turned to look at the man. Sincerity seemed to bleed from every pore in his body, but the Executioner had known some extremely talented and convincing con men in his day. He'd trust this man—to a point—but he planned on keeping one eye on Kunkle for a while, ready for any surprises the detective might have up his sleeve. "Just one other thing," he finally said.

"What's that, Mr. Cooper?"

"Be *very* careful where you point your gun when we get into the next firefight."

"I will," Kunkle promised.

"Good," Bolan said. "Because if I so much as suspect it might be aimed at me, I'll drop you where you stand."

Reaching into his jacket, Bolan pulled out the cell phone he'd taken from Jackson's body. "Take this one, and the phone you have from Westbrook, and dump them both," he said. "First see if there were any calls to McFarley's number over the last few hours. I can't imagine that Jake was telling us the truth."

Kunkle took the phone from Bolan, pulled out the one he already had and went to work as the soldier drove on. He was nearing the outskirts of New Orleans, and had just come over a small rise, when he spotted the parish deputy sheriff's vehicle parked on the other side of the road. A radar gun was pointed out the window, and Bolan's eyes automatically dropped to the speedometer. He was five miles under the limit, so there should be no problems here.

Shouldn't be, he realized as he watched the marked unit

pull the radar gun back into the vehicle and roll forward into a U-turn. But it looked like there was going to be.

Bolan waited until the red lights came on. There was no way he was going to outrun the parish vehicle in the ancient pickup, so he slowed, pulling the pickup over to the side of the road.

In addition to the cell phones, Kunkle also had his police credentials out in his lap. "I can badge us out of this," he said. "No problem."

"I don't think it's going to be that simple," Bolan said as they pulled to a stop. "I wasn't speeding, which means this deputy stopped us for some other reason." He watched the uniformed officer in the car behind him get out, his hand unsnapping the retaining strap on his sidearm. With the same hand on the weapon's grip, he walked slowly forward.

When the man had reached the driver's side of the pickup, Bolan could see that he carried a Beretta 92—not much different from his own 93-R, but lacking the 3-shot-burst mode and the fold-down front grip. It shot the same deadly 9 mm rounds, however. And the Executioner knew he was going to have to play this situation cool.

Bolan didn't kill cops. He was on the same side as they were, and it violated his own personal creed.

"Driver's license, registration and proof of insurance," the deputy said, his eyes taking in Bolan and moving on to Kunkle. Clipped to his uniform blouse, opposite his badge, was the name Frantz.

Bolan slowly retrieved the counterfeit Justice Department badge case from his inside jacket pocket. Keeping the badge hidden from the deputy's eyes, he pulled out a driver's license identifying him as Matt Cooper. As he handed the license through the window, he heard Kunkle rummaging around in the glove compartment for the other documents.

Deputy Frantz stared hard at the picture on the license,

then back at Bolan's face. "Is this your vehicle, Mr. Cooper?" he asked.

Bolan knew the registration and insurance papers would not be in his name. So he responded with, "No, we just borrowed it from a friend back at the marina."

"What's the friend's name?" Frantz asked.

Kunkle had found the papers he was looking for and hurriedly answered for Bolan. "Jesse Durrosset," he said, leaning across Bolan to hand the deputy the documents.

Frantz stared down at the papers for a second, then suddenly stuck them into his back pocket and drew his gun. "Both of you!" he shouted in a deep voice filled with authority. "Keep your hands where I can see them and get out of the vehicle."

Bolan raised his hands, as did Kunkle.

"You first," the deputy ordered the detective. "Get out on your side, keep your hands in the air and walk around the front of the pickup."

Kunkle opened the door and got out. Keeping his hands high and in sight, he said, "I'm telling you, Deputy, we just borrowed this pickup from Jesse."

The deputy kept his pistol on the detective as the man walked around the truck. "Oh, really?" he said in a sarcastic tone. "Well, it just so happens that Jesse Durrosset is my second cousin, and he wouldn't loan this truck to God if He asked to borrow it. It's been his 'baby' for twenty years, and nobody drives it but him."

Bolan didn't respond, silently calculating his next move.

The deputy sheriff continued. "Now get down on the ground and interlace your fingers behind your head."

As Kunkle complied, Bolan glanced from the deputy's face to the Beretta 92. He could almost reach the gun from where he sat, but he calculated that he would be a few inches short unless he lunged chest-deep through the driver's window.

And that might just give Deputy Frantz the time it took to react.

And pull back to shoot him.

"All right, now it's your turn," Frantz said, turning back to Bolan as he took another step back from the pickup. "Keep your hands up. Reach through the window and open the door from the outside."

"Just before you two topped that hill," Deputy Frantz said as he shoved Bolan up against the side of the pickup, "I got a call about shots being fired back at the marina. Then here you come in Jesse's truck, which he never loans out. Am I supposed to think that's just a coincidence?"

Bolan felt the muzzle of the Beretta 92 in the small of his back as Deputy Frantz started at the collar, patting him down for weapons with his other hand. That was a mistake. It let the soldier know exactly where the deputy's gun was.

Bolan also knew it was only a matter of seconds before the man found his sound-suppressed Beretta, and the .44 Magnum Desert Eagle. And neither of the two weapons looked anything like a fellow cop's gun. If Frantz overacted, Bolan and Kunkle might take bullets simply from the deputy's nervousness.

It was time to act.

As Deputy Frantz's left hand finished running the length of Bolan's arm and started toward his armpit, the Executioner made his move. Twisting violently, he swept the Beretta 92 to his side. The weapon discharged a few inches from his body as Frantz pulled the trigger. But before he could react further, Bolan had sent the same right cross that had felled the heavyweight fighter, Jackson, into the man's chin.

Frantz was out cold before he fell to the asphalt next to the pickup.

Kunkle got up from the ground. "Nice punch," he said, hurriedly grabbing Frantz's Beretta and then pulling a backup piece—a .38 S&W Chief's Special—from the unconscious man's Wellington boot. "Although I feel a little bit like a dog chasing cars. What does he do with the car if it stops?"

Bolan already had the answer. Frantz had fallen onto his back. The soldier rolled him over, pulling a set of handcuffs from a pouch on the back of the deputy's black Sam Browne belt. Quickly, he rolled him over again and cuffed the deputy behind his back, then lifted him in a fireman's carry and walked him to the backseat of the patrol car.

"We're just going to leave him out here?" Kunkle asked.

Bolan hurried back to the spot where Frantz had been and picked up the cowboy hat, which had fallen from his head. "No," he said, placing it atop his own head. "He was liable to have radioed in to report the stop while the lights were flashing. If he did, then every other cop in the area will have the word about 'Cousin Jesse's' pickup. And some other cousin, or nephew, or brother-in-law, or uncle might stop us again down the road."

Kunkle laughed.

"So we're going to take Deputy Frantz on a ride back to New Orleans in his own vehicle. That's why I'm wearing this." Bolan shoved the cowboy hat harder onto his head, then opened the driver's door of the black-and-white patrol car and slid behind the wheel, hunching down slightly to obscure most of his upper body. "Go get the ice chest," he ordered Kunkle.

Kunkle hurried back to the pickup and returned with the chest. He didn't have to be told to get in on the passenger's side again.

"We'll dump this vehicle with Frantz in it as soon as we hit town and can find other transport," Bolan said. "All that'll be hurt is the deputy's pride."

"I'd say his chin might ache a little, too," Kunkle said as Bolan pulled the patrol car around the old pickup and started down the asphalt once more. "At least for a while. What do we do if he comes around again before we're through with the car?"

Bolan held up a big right fist. "I have more anesthetic," he said simply, then floored the accelerator and sped on. "By the way, were there any calls from Jake and his partner to McFarley?" he asked Kunkle.

"Only about a dozen," Kunkle said. "From both phones." He rested an arm on the ice chest on the seat between them. "We're going to have to come up with some kind of story as to why you took me out of O'Brien's and brought me out to the marina."

"What do you mean, *we?*" the Executioner asked. "You're dead, remember?"

"Okay, I meant *you'll* have to come up with a story," Kunkle said.

"I can cover it. But if you're going to be hanging around me, we're going to have to change your appearance, and you can't ever be with me when I'm with McFarley or any of his other goons who know you."

Kunkle nodded. "That can be worked out," he said. "Besides, most of the men who knew me by sight are already dead. I only dealt with, and got paid by, the top men in the organization. Before you even came on the scene I'd gotten word that McFarley killed Jo-Jo Gau. And the man you shot back at the marina with Jake was Razor Westbrook, another top gunman and enforcer."

"I'd met him," Bolan said. "He and another goon were at McFarley's when I had dinner there night before last."

"Right," Kunkle said. "That would have been Felix O'Banion. As far as I know, he's the only other one of McFarley's men who knows me by sight. But I can't be sure."

"Then we need to err on the side of safety," Bolan said. "Have you spent any time out at the mansion?"

Kunkle nodded, his face turning slightly red with shame. "Yeah," he said. "I've been to McFarley's office a time or two, and I've spent a little time with some of the girls on the floors below the office, too."

"They'll know you then," Bolan said. "And while I'm still keeping an eye on you to see if your change of heart is genuine, I think we've reached a point where you can drop the 'Mr. Cooper' name."

"Matt?" Kunkle asked.

Bolan turned toward him and stared hard into the man's face. "Make it 'Cooper,'" he said. "We'll keep working toward 'Matt.'"

Kunkle let a small smile curl the corner of his lips. "Okay, Cooper," he said.

And then the two men who had first escaped death, and then imprisonment, drove on in silence toward the city of New Orleans.

BOLAN TOOK THE ELEVATOR to the top floor of the old mansion-bordello, the ice chest cradled in both arms. He had sensed no tension when he'd entered on the ground floor, but he knew he was taking another calculated risk by even returning to McFarley's place.

He'd have to assume that the phone calls from Jackson and Westbrook had informed the New Orleans crime boss that "Matt Cooper" had taken Kunkle out of Pat O'Brien's without violence, and that the two men had passed on the information that they'd taken a cab out of the city to the marina. At that point, he was going to have to "twist" the story to fit whatever intel Westbrook and Jackson had relayed back to their boss via their cell phones.

He'd have to think on his feet. And fast. Somehow, he had to get McFarley to reveal as much of what he already knew as he could, then fill in the gaps of the story.

Bolan would emphasize three things. First, it hadn't made sense to kill the police detective in front of witnesses in O'Brien's. Second, the marina was empty during the wee hours of the morning, and third, alligators were a perfect way to get rid of a body.

The part of the story Bolan didn't yet know how to cover was his connection to the boat. Jackson and Westbrook had probably seen the ice chest being off-loaded when they returned to the dock. If they'd reported that to McFarley, Bolan was going to have to come up with a reasonable explanation.

And so far, he hadn't been able to do that.

The elevator reached the top floor and Bolan stepped out to be greeted by the other Irishman—Felix O'Banion. O'Banion motioned for the soldier to put the ice chest on the floor, then turn and put his hands on the wall. Bolan complied. Carefully patting him down, O'Banion came first to the Beretta 93-R in the shoulder rig. Jerking it out of its holster, he stared down at the sound suppressor on the end.

After stuffing the weapon into his belt, O'Banion's hands moved on. When he found the Desert Eagle on Bolan's hip, he pulled it out as well. "Mother McGee!" he said as he stared at the giant .44 Magnum pistol. "You don't take any chances, do you, boyo?"

"Not when I don't have to," Bolan said. "But I'm not sure why you're going through all this again. Surely your boss didn't expect me to kill Kunkle bare-handed."

O'Banion's hands went back to work, checking Bolan's crotch area more carefully this time. When he found nothing there, he said, "So you didn't bring your little wheel gun this time?"

"I figured the .44 and 9 mm were enough," Bolan said. In his mind's eye, however, he pictured the .22 Magnum Pug pressed against his back by the twin-magazine caddy. O'Banion's hands had passed over it twice during the search and missed it both times.

Showing McFarley that he had slipped the hidden .22 Magnum pistol through his security had served a purpose,

earlier. But this time, it would be better that the crime boss
and his minions didn't know all of his secrets.

When O'Banion had finally located and removed the Cold
Steel Espada fighting knife from Bolan's waistband, he said,
"Let's go on to the office."

"When do I get my guns and knife back?" Bolan asked as
he picked up the ice chest once more.

"When McFarley says you do," O'Banion said bluntly. He
led the way down the hall.

Bolan followed, carrying the ice chest. He wasn't sure
exactly what the pecking order had been around here, but
with Jo-Jo Gau, Jackson and Westbrook dead, it looked like
O'Banion was McFarley's number-one goon. He probably had
been all along, considering the fact that McFarley had brought
him all the way from Ireland. But in any case, the upper ech-
elon of McFarley's criminal empire was thinning out fast.

Which should make the Irishman even more anxious to use
Cooper's skills.

O'Banion came to McFarley's office, knocked twice, then
opened the door. He stepped back to let Bolan through, then
entered and closed the door behind him.

McFarley sat in his desk chair, his feet crossed and rest-
ing on the desktop. "Need a hand or two?" Bolan asked as
he entered the room.

"Extremely funny." McFarley looked sternly at Bolan and
said, "Put it on my desk."

Bolan complied, then stepped back away from the desk.

O'Banion's hands and arms were full of the Executioner's
weapons. He stepped forward and set them on the desk next
to the ice chest.

McFarley chuckled. "You don't travel light, do you?" he
said.

Bolan saw no reason to answer.

McFarley opened the ice chest lid and took a quick look
at the contents. Then he closed it again and motioned for

O'Banion to take it. "We'll run the prints and find out if it's really Kunkle," he said. "If it turns out that the hands are his, I'll give you your toys back." He gestured toward the pile of weapons on his desk. "But while we're waiting, there are a few things we need to clear up." He opened a drawer in his desk, and Bolan watched as he pulled out a British Webley revolver with pearl grips. Aiming the big .455 at the soldier, he said, "Where's the rest of Kunkle's body?"

"In an alligator's intestinal tract by now," Bolan said simply.

"You shoot him?" McFarley demanded.

Bolan's face took on a deadpan expression. "Nope," he said. "As I'm sure you know, gators like to kill their own find. That's why I knocked him out, sawed off his hands and then fed him to the big lizard before he could bleed out."

The Webley stayed trained on Bolan. "I haven't heard from Jackson or my other man, Westbrook," McFarley said. "They were following you."

"I know that," Bolan said. "And I'd be pretty surprised if you did hear from them again. Ever."

"Why's that?" McFarley asked, pulling his feet off the desk.

Bolan stared him in the eyes. "Because I killed them both."

McFarley smoothed out the wrinkles in his slacks and leaned inward, the Webley still pointed at Bolan. "Why?" he asked. "You weren't even supposed to see them. I ordered them to stay back out of sight and report on your actions."

Bolan laughed. "Well, that's not what they did," he said. "It sounds like both of them shooting Uzis at me violated your orders. I didn't have much choice."

By this point, O'Banion had carried the ice chest out of the office, but McFarley looked toward the door where he'd last been. "What was the ice chest doing on the boat?" he demanded, his knuckles whitening around the pearl grips of the Webley.

There it was. The weak spot in Bolan's story. Jackson and Westbrook *had* seen him and Kunkle take the ice chest off the boat, and they'd told McFarley.

Bolan had no choice but to gamble. "Ice chest off what boat?" he said.

McFarley was still staring him in the eye. "They called in and told me that you and Kunkle took an ice chest off an air-boat. And that Kunkle was still alive, and looked like he was helping you instead of getting his hands cut off and preparing to become Purina Alligator Chow."

Bolan laughed again. "Well, guys who'd violate your orders not to shoot us just might stoop to telling a lie now and then, don't you think?" he said. "Jake was pissed off at me because I kicked his ass twice yesterday. Sounds to me like he convinced Westbrook to come up with a story that would be a good reason to kill me." Bolan paused. "I don't know anything about a boat. I took the ice chest with me."

"In a cab?" McFarley asked.

"Yes, in a cab," Bolan came back. "This is New Orleans, Tommy," he said. "In the wake of Hurricane Katrina, cabbies have seen far stranger things than being asked to drive two men to a marina with an ice chest."

McFarley leaned yet closer and his eyes narrowed. "I'm not sure I'm buying all of this, Cooper," he said. "How did you get Kunkle out of O'Brien's without a fight?"

"By showing him that little .22 Magnum you saw the other day," Bolan said.

"And what story did you give him that made him cooperate in going to the marina?" McFarley demanded.

"I told him you wanted a final drug pickup escorted into town in safety. After that was over, you'd respect his new-found religion and leave him alone."

"It's hard to believe he'd buy a story like that," McFarley said.

"Men will believe almost anything if they want to bad enough," Bolan said.

Slowly, McFarley nodded. "Okay," he said. "I'll know more when the fingerprint results come back. But if it turns out you did your job, you've earned a spot on the starting lineup. I had to kill my man Gau. You took out Westbrook. The only heavy hitter I've got left is O'Banion." His eyes narrowed even further as the Webley continued to point at Bolan. "Of course if you're trying to pull some trick…" His voice trailed off. But a few seconds later he finished with, "You'll be alligator bait yourself."

"That sounds fair enough to me," Bolan said.

"Then sit down," McFarley said, "and wait." He put his feet back up on his desk and leaned back in his chair again. "It shouldn't take long. We've got a great fingerprint contact inside the NOPD, and that AFIS system is really helpful." He laughed at the irony of the Advanced Fingerprint Identification System making *his* work easier as well as that of the police.

Bolan turned toward the chairs against the wall opposite McFarley's desk. Sometime since he'd been there last, someone had cleaned the blood and brains off the wall. He dropped into one of the chairs. As he waited, he thought back to his actions after he and Kunkle had taken the police car. They had passed several other parish deputy cars heading out to the scene of the gunfight. With Frantz's cowboy hat pulled down low over his eyes, the Executioner had exchanged waves with the drivers coming toward him. A few radio transmissions had come for them, but Bolan had ignored them. By the time the other deputies figured out something was amiss, he knew he'd have ditched the patrol car with Deputy Frantz still handcuffed in the backseat.

And that was exactly what had happened. Bolan had driven on into New Orleans, then spotted a small shopping center a block from a low-rent hotel. He had let Kunkle out in front of a drug store amid the other businesses with orders to pick up the items he needed to change his appearance. When he'd done that, the reborn detective was to walk to the hotel, rent a room, then leave his necktie around the doorknob so Bolan could find him without going through the desk clerk.

While Kunkle did all this, Bolan would take the severed hands to McFarley, then return to the hotel at the first opportunity.

Bolan and McFarley sat silently in the office. Roughly fifteen minutes after the soldier had taken his seat, O'Banion opened the office door, stuck his head inside, then glanced from Bolan to McFarley. Finally, he nodded. "They're Kunkle's hands," he said.

McFarley's mood changed instantly from skeptical to a satisfied, bordering on excited. "Good work, Cooper," he said, pulling his feet off the desk and standing up. He extended his right hand across the desk.

Bolan moved from the wall and shook it.

"Stay in here, O'Banion," McFarley called out before the other Irishman could shut the door again.

O'Banion stepped inside.

"From now on," McFarley said, "Cooper's taking the place of Gau and Westbrook."

"That's one man taking the place of two," O'Banion said. "He can't—"

McFarley didn't let him finish. "It appears to me that Cooper can do the work of two of you," he said sharply. "And until I find another capable man, you'll both just have to make up for the slack." He had kept his grip on Bolan's hand but then dropped it.

"I've got another assignment for you, Cooper," he said, "but you've been up all night. You need a little rest first?"

Bolan thought of Kunkle. By this point, the man should have checked into the hotel down the block from the shopping center. He still wasn't thoroughly convinced that the detective had experienced a true conversion to Christianity, and he needed to check up on him. "It wouldn't hurt anything," Bolan finally said. "I'm not at my best."

"Well, you're going to need to be at your best for what I have for you next," McFarley said. "So…how about you go downstairs, pick out a room and I'll send a couple of girls in to help you relax before you nod off?" His voice had taken on a tone as sleazy as the hotel where Kunkle was waiting.

Bolan chuckled. "I appreciate the gesture," he said. "But I sleep better when I'm on my own."

McFarley frowned. "You want to go back to your condo?" he asked with a small amount of the skepticism returning to his voice.

"I do," Bolan said. "It's a place where I can close my eyes without worrying about jealous employees of yours like Jake trying to kill me." He glanced toward O'Banion, making it obvious that he didn't trust the man.

McFarley nodded. "Okay," he said. "I don't particularly like it, but I can understand it. You've pretty much proved yourself to me, Cooper. Now I suppose we've got to prove ourselves to you."

Turning to O'Banion himself, he said, "Felix, let Cooper go and make sure nobody tails him this time. If anything— anything at all—happens to him, the same thing's going to happen to you. You understand?"

O'Banion didn't like it, but he nodded.

McFarley held out his hand again and Bolan shook it once more. "I've got a feeling we're going to go places, you and me," the New Orleans kingpin said. "So go catch a few hours of sleep. I've got one more sort of 'test' job for you before I trust you a hundred percent. It's a bit unusual, but I want to see how you handle it." The New Orleans pimp and racketeer went on to give him a few details of the next job.

And Bolan had to admit, it *was* unusual.

The Executioner nodded his understanding. He had a few

questions about this final so-called test job, but he thought it better not to ask at this point.

"Is there anything else you need before you go?" McFarley asked.

"I could use a vehicle," Bolan said. "I'm getting sick of cabs. And I'm also getting sick of wondering which cabbies might remember me to the police later on."

"Felix," McFarley said, "take him down to the parking lot and fix him up. Something good but not too flashy." He smiled at Bolan. "We don't want him attracting too much attention." Then, without further words, he nodded toward the Beretta and Desert Eagle on his desk.

Bolan holstered both of his guns. Then, with a final glance at McFarley, he walked out of the room, down the hall and rode the elevator to the ground floor with O'Banion.

And a few minutes later, the Executioner was driving away in a nearly new Cadillac Escalade.

9

The drugstore was just opening as Kunkle got out of the deputy sheriff's car. He waited as the man inside the glass door pulled a ring of keys from his belt and inserted one into the lock. A moment later, he became the store's first customer of the day.

In his mind, Kunkle tried to picture how he could change his appearance to the fullest, but he didn't try to kid himself. No matter what he did, anyone within McFarley's circle of crime who had known him before would recognize him again. At least close up. The cold hard fact was that if there was any doubt left in the New Orleans crime kingpin's mind as to his death, they'd all be looking for him. And *expecting* him to try to change his looks.

Kunkle grabbed a small basket from the stack next to the entrance and proceeded into the store. Above his head, he saw a sign on the aisle against the wall that read Shaving Products. He walked slowly down the side of the store, picking up a package of disposable razors and a can of shaving cream.

Should he shave his face and head? Maybe. That would make for the most dramatic change between his longish hair and beard. But it would also be the most obvious if anyone in McFarley's power structure was in the least bit suspicious. Perhaps there was a better way.

In the far corner of the store, Kunkle saw an unusual-looking item called a HeadBlade. Stopping in front of the display, he pulled one off the rack and looked closer. He might need it. The device came with several extra cartridges and he dropped one into his basket.

Moving along the back wall of the store, Kunkle looked up to see a variety of electric hair clippers. He had been lucky so far, and whatever gene had caused his father to go bald by his age seemed to have skipped him. But on this day, he needed a different look, and he reached up and pulled down a cardboard box that read Wahl. It came with attachments that ranged by eight of an inch lengths from one-eighth to one inch. The detective laughed inwardly. It would do. And he would have a new look to go along with the new life he was beginning.

Kunkle thought about that new life as he moved to the next aisle over marked Hair Care. Ever since he had attended the revival meeting featuring the son of a world-famous evangelist, he'd felt like a different man. He had found himself leaning forward in his seat and focusing on what the man was saying. Suddenly, as if he'd been hit by lightning, Kunkle had developed a conscience, which brought on a wave of guilt as powerful as the winds that had swirled around Hurricane Katrina.

As the sermon went on, Kunkle had begun to realize that he could not go on being a dishonest cop, or committing the other sins that were part of his lifestyle. And with that realization came a new and strange conflict of emotions. He continued to feel guilt about all of the bribes he'd taken, and the times he'd looked the other way when McFarley's men had committed crimes. But along with that guilt—and in seeming contrast to it—came a newfound joy that he had never before experienced.

Kunkle had been saved. At some point during that sermon, he had begun to realize just how lost he had become. And as he listened to the preacher he had felt tears forming in his eyes. When the invitation to accept Christ as his personal savior came at the end of the service, Kunkle had been surprised to find himself joining dozens of others in the aisles, walking toward the front of the huge stadium. He had received some literature, and a small copy of the New Testament, as had the others. Looking around he had seen that some people were crying. Others appeared to be in shock. But all looked sincere about giving their hearts to Jesus.

And they would have to have been, Kunkle thought as he picked up a small box of hair-bleach and dropped it in his basket. What other possible explanation could there be for publicly humiliating themselves like that?

The New Orleans detective grabbed a small tube of hair-dressing gel and added it to his other items. He paused in front of a bin piled high with plastic bags bearing elastic hair bands. A new thought as to how he might change his appearance entered his head, and he picked up one of the bags.

As he started toward the front of the store and the cash register, Kunkle's mind raced back to the man he had talked to right after the revival meeting. He had never gotten his name, but he remembered that the man said he was a deacon in one of the local churches. And he had invited Kunkle to that church the next Sunday. Kunkle had gone, and once again he had found himself walking down the aisle at the end of the service. Not to announce his salvation publicly—he'd already done that—but to rededicate his life to the service of Jesus Christ. He would become an honest cop, even if that meant being arrested and jailed himself for his past crimes. Regardless of what came his way, he intended to serve the Lord as best he could for the rest of his life.

A rush of joy came over Kunkle, covering the guilt for a moment as he neared the cash register. He had talked to other

Christians after that service, and learned that he would probably feel some guilt for a while, if not from then on. But he
had been saved from eternal damnation, and just knowing
that was worth any amount of guilt that came with it.

A smile broke out on the detective's face as he stopped at
the cash register. It had to have been catching because the
teenage girl behind the counter gave him a big smile back. As
she rang up his items, Kunkle realized suddenly that he had
not checked out her breasts, posterior, or any other parts of
her body. The automatic lust he had always felt when meeting
a new female simply wasn't there. Not that he didn't know she
was attractive—he did. But in the place of lust he found that
he was filled with love. Not a romantic or sexual love, but just
a simple love for a fellow human being.

Kunkle came close to asking the girl if she knew Jesus.
But he hadn't quite reached that point yet, and he paid her
with the money Matt Cooper had given him, took the plastic
bag she handed him, then simply smiled again as he left the
drugstore.

A Goodwill store was adjacent to the drugstore, and
Kunkle entered quickly, grabbing two used pairs of denim
jeans and a handful of T-shirts in his size. He paid for them
and left.

The Hotel Lafitte was only a block-and-a-half away, and
Kunkle breathed in the humid air of New Orleans as he
passed the other stores in the small shopping center that were
just opening for business. He noticed that many of the people
he passed on the sidewalk were smiling, and realized that was
because he, himself, wore a big broad grin. It was a new experience for him, and one he liked. A wave of guilt rolled over
him but passed. He remembered what the preacher had said at
the revival.

*He couldn't change his past. But he could certainly change
his future.*

Kunkle pushed through the door to the hotel office and

walked to the front desk. The place had a greasy feel to it and gave him the urge to take a shower. The Lafitte was widely known in the NOPD as a hangout for crack addicts, other drug abusers and prostitutes. But strangely enough, Kunkle had never worked a case that brought him there before.

Was that just luck? he wondered. Or had there been something else at work? Something that saw a bigger picture than he ever could? Something that had kept his face from being known at the Hotel Lafitte so he could check in at this moment in anonymity?

Was it God at work?

Kunkle didn't know, but he knew that two weeks ago, such a thought would have never crossed his mind.

An emaciated man with needle tracks on both arms appeared from a door behind the desk. Kunkle caught himself thinking, there but for the grace of God go I. Instead of the usual revulsion he would have expected to feel, he found himself sympathizing with the man and wondering what life had thrown his way that caused him to turn to drugs as an escape. It was a new and strange reaction for the hardened New Orleans detective, and it perplexed him.

As he moved toward the pitiful man at the check-in counter, he heard a mumbled voice ask, "You want it by the hour, day, or week?" Kunkle noted that the man's eyes were glazed over as if his mind were somewhere far away. No crackhead here, he thought. The skinny remembrance of a man was on heroin. "I'll take a week," he replied, then handed over a hundred-dollar bill and got a twenty back in change.

"Room 307," the heroin addict mumbled and pointed toward the ceiling. "Top floor."

Kunkle jammed the twenty-dollar bill into his pants pocket and started toward the elevator. He stopped when he saw the scrawled Out of Order sign taped to the doors. It was curling at the edges and looked like it had been there for weeks.

Turning toward the stairs, the reborn New Orleans detective started up the steps. He had work to do. God's work. And the sooner he finished changing his looks the sooner he could get back with Cooper and get it done.

When he reached the third floor, he found room 307, then unknotted his necktie and looped it over the doorknob so Cooper would know which room he was in.

Then he opened the door, and with the shaving cream, razor and other items he'd bought at the drugstore in hand, Kunkle headed into the bathroom.

10

Bolan pulled the Cadillac Escalade into the parking lot of the Hotel Lafitte, stopping it at the other end of the lot from the front office. A rear entrance to the building was right in front of him. But before he took it, he had one more security duty to perform.

He had heard McFarley order O'Banion to make sure no one tailed him this time. But he couldn't be sure that hadn't been said just to throw him off guard. The transplanted Irish crime boss could have always reversed that order as soon as he was out of earshot, and while the Irishman had as much as told Bolan that he now trusted him, the assignment he had been given hinted otherwise. Compared to the other irons McFarley had in the fire, the mission he'd sent Bolan on seemed like mere child's play.

The soldier killed the engine and withdrew the key. It was a strange situation in which he found himself. McFarley was still testing him for trustworthiness. At the same time, he was testing Kunkle. And neither Bolan nor McFarley was completely convinced yet.

Bolan started in the front seat, searching every nook and cranny of the Escalade, but he found no tracking device of any kind. When he had finished with the front, he climbed over the seat and searched the back. Again, nothing.

Getting out of the Escalade, he walked to the back bumper. Nothing was hidden below it. Just to make sure, he dropped to the ground and began scooting beneath the vehicle, holding a small ASP flashlight in his teeth as he checked the underside of the Caddie.

Yet again, he found no devices to assist anyone trying to follow him.

Emerging from below the front bumper, Bolan stood up and brushed himself off. A moment later, he entered the Hotel Lafitte through the rear entrance and began circling the first floor, looking for a necktie on the doorknobs. The smell of marijuana was strong in the hall air, emanating from several of the rooms. But he saw no necktie.

Bolan climbed the steps to the second floor, the odor of marijuana being replaced by the wretched smell of vomit on the stairs. Again, he circled the floor. But again, he saw no tie.

Room 307 was just to the right of the staircase and Bolan spotted the tie the moment he set foot on the hotel's top floor. He knocked three times, then unwound the tie from the doorknob. A moment later, he saw the peephole darken, and then the door began to swing back open.

Kunkle stepped back from the door to let him enter.

"I wouldn't have recognized you if I didn't already know you," Bolan said as he walked past the man into the shabby room. "On the other hand, the old saying, 'Even your mother wouldn't recognize you' doesn't apply." He stopped to scrutinize Kunkle more closely. "We can't ever forget that that goes for everyone else who knows you, too. We still need to keep you out of sight around anyone associated with McFarley. Or at least at a safe distance." Bolan handed the necktie to the detective.

The soldier walked on past the man and grabbed a rickety

chair in front of an equally worn-out desk. Turning it backward, he rested his arms on the back of the chair and waited while Kunkle took a seat on the edge of the frayed bedspread. The detective really *had* changed his appearance to the maximum. He had shaved the top of his head to the skull but left the hair on the sides and back hanging straight and long. Instead of the full beard he had formerly worn, he now had long mutton-chop sideburns that extended well below his ears. And his beard had been trimmed into a short, neat goatee and mustache. All of the hair that was left—both head and face—had been bleached blond from its former dark brown, and the back had been long enough to be tied into a short ponytail.

Instead of the crumpled suit he had worn earlier, Kunkle now had on a plain white T-shirt, faded blue jeans and well-worn blue-and-white athletic shoes.

"It's a new look for a new life," Kunkle said. He paused, and Bolan could almost feel his stare as he waited for a reaction. When the Executioner didn't give him one, he went on. "I know you still aren't convinced that I'm sincere, Cooper, and I don't blame you. I'll just have to keep proving it to you until you believe me."

"I'm getting closer," Bolan said simply.

Kunkle nodded. "Before we go on, I've got a couple of questions, if you don't mind."

"Hit me with them," Bolan said.

"I know you're one of the 'good guys,'" the detective said. "Probably a Fed. But can you tell me what branch you're with?"

"No," Bolan said. "Let me just tell you that I've got an unusual arrangement with the government, that I'm on the side of justice, and we'll leave it at that."

Kunkle nodded again. "Okay. But I also get the feeling that you don't mind working outside the law for a greater purpose. Am I right there?"

"You are," the soldier said. "I don't mind breaking little

laws to catch big bad guys." He paused a moment, then added, "And when I've caught them, I don't mind breaking big laws to stop them."

"Then here's the big question, I guess," Kunkle said. "You've already got access to McFarley. Why not just kill him right now and get it over with?"

Bolan uncrossed his arms, held them out to his side to stretch the muscles, then crossed them again. "I've considered that," he said. "But McFarley has operations in a lot of different areas. Drug smuggling, gunrunning, fixing boxing matches, and others. I need to disrupt at least a few of these activities before McFarley goes down. If I don't, someone else will just step in and take his place."

Kunkle shrugged. "Makes sense to me."

"Make no mistake," the Executioner said. "I plan to rid this planet of Tommy McFarley, but I've got to save him for later."

Silence fell over the room for a few seconds while Kunkle let the information sink into his brain. Then Bolan broke that silence, changing the subject with, "You ever hear of a guy named Bill Dill?"

Kunkle laughed out loud. "Are you kidding?" he said. "Next to McFarley himself, Dill is the biggest racketeer in New Orleans." He paused for a moment, and Bolan saw the question in his eyes before he put it into one simple word.

"Why?" the detective asked.

"Because I've just been assigned to burglarize his place," Bolan said. "And you're coming with me on the job."

Kunkle's laugh became more of a snort. "That's not surprising. Bill Dill and McFarley hate each other's guts. They're in direct competition." He stopped talking for a moment, then said, "Let me go out on a limb here and guess what McFarley wants. Dill's New York Jets collection."

Bolan was slightly surprised. "Right on the money," he said. "But how could you have known that?"

Kunkle's laugh faded to a low chuckle. "It's pretty much

common knowledge within the criminal circles of New Orleans that Dill's a big Jets fan. In fact, he's probably the only man in Louisiana who doesn't root for the Saints." He stopped talking for a moment and scratched his face where he'd shaved it between one mutton-chop sideburn and his goatee. "You see, Dill was born and raised in New York. I've never seen it, but it's reputed that he's got this collection of Jets paraphernalia that dates back to Super Bowl III. Supposed to be worth over two million in autographed pictures and other things."

"That's pretty much what McFarley told me," Bolan said. "And there's a rumor that he has Joe Namath's Super Bowl ring."

Kunkle shook his new ponytail and let it flap back and forth behind his head like a horse swatting flies. "That rumor's been around for years," he said. "Dill supposedly hired some top-notch New York burglar to break into Namath's apartment. I don't doubt that. What I doubt is that he actually got the ring."

"Why's that?" Bolan asked.

"Because it would have made the news if he had," Kunkle came back. "That's not something Broadway Joe would have taken sitting down. Besides, if I had a Super Bowl ring, I'd even wear it when I slept, wouldn't you?"

Bolan didn't respond.

"But there's another rumor about that whole incident," Kunkle said. "And it's just possible that it's true. The way it goes is that Dill's man *did* get Namath's ring, but Joe kept the whole thing quiet. Why is anybody's guess. But in this story, Namath just had a duplicate made." The detective snorted. "The man's certainly got the money for it," he finished.

Bolan nodded, then said, "According to McFarley, there's yet one more version of this legend. McFarley's convinced that Dill *did* hire the burglar, but the guy wasn't as good as he'd thought. According to Tommy, he got caught, pled out for a deal with the District Attorney's Office up there, and Namath got the ring back."

"Is it the ring McFarley is after?" Kunkle asked. "For a Jets fan, it would be like the Holy Grail. And it sounds like something McFarley would want just to sort of spit in Dill's face."

"He specified the ring, if it's there," Bolan said. "He isn't sure Dill has it, either, but he wants as much of the other Jets paraphernalia as we can carry out, too. It's not the monetary worth of the fan gear that McFarley's looking for. You were right—it's just to spit in Dill's face. He wants to take the Jets fan's favorite toys away from him and make sure the man, and everyone else in New Orleans, knows where they went."

"There are aspects of all this that sound fishy to me," Kunkle said, frowning as he stood up from the bed and walked toward the bathroom "It sounds like McFarley is still trying to decide if he can trust you just like you're trying to decide if you can trust me."

"That's exactly what it is," Bolan said as the other man turned and paced back toward him. "There have been too many 'explanations' that went with your supposed murder. Like killing Jake and Razor Westbrook. And the fact that those two had told McFarley the ice chest came off a boat. But I think we've caught a bit of luck on this one."

"How's that?" Kunkle asked as he sat back down on the edge of the bed.

"This is a simple burglary," Bolan said. "If we pull it off right, we can go through with the whole thing exactly as ordered with no 'surprises' to explain."

He reached into the inside pocket of his jacket and pulled out a thin cardboard paper folded into fourths. "I'm not sure how McFarley got this," he told Kunkle. "He must have somebody on the inside of Dill's operation. But, whatever the situation, he gave me this hand-drawn map of Dill's house." He stood up and walked to the table next to the sliding glass door that led to the third-floor porch. Then, unfolding the cardboard, he spread it out on the table.

"McFarley's undoubtedly got snitches inside city and county government," the detective said. "He might have someone in the county assessor's office."

"Maybe," Bolan said. "But this thing is obviously amateurish. And whoever drew it for him has written on it, naming the rooms." He turned the thick paper sideways so both he and Kunkle could read it. "Here's what Dill calls the Family Room. And the Conservatory. There's a star up here on the second floor of the Study. That's where McFarley believes the Jets collection is."

Kunkle frowned at the plans. "McFarley's had somebody inside the house," he finally said. "Probably somebody who's on Dill's payroll but getting a little extra cash from McFarley."

"Yeah," Bolan said. "But that's not our concern at the moment. What we need to do is figure out the safest way in and out of the house. To get to the Study, we've got to go right through Dill's bedroom. With him and his wife sleeping not two feet away from the short hall that leads to it." He glanced at Kunkle's face and saw the indecision on it. "What's wrong?" he asked.

Kunkle's frown deepened. "I'm not sure how I feel about stealing an honest collection," he said. "After all, I'm trying to turn over a new leaf."

"The collection may be honest," Bolan said. "But the man who owns it isn't. If he was, I wouldn't feel right about stealing from him, either. But Bill Dill is a criminal who's just as bad as McFarley. Just not quite as successful. So I don't feel bad about ripping off two million dollars' worth of autographs and pennants from him."

"It's still stealing," Kunkle said softly.

Bolan stared deep into the man's eyes. Behind them, he saw a soul in turmoil, a man going through a transformation from the evil life he'd been leading into a more moral existence. And the process was confusing the detective.

Bolan couldn't afford to leave such confusion in Kunkle's brain. Confusion brought about hesitation, and hesitation could get both of them killed.

"Let me put this in terms you might understand better," Bolan said. "Do you think it would be right, or wrong, to go into a church, tear it up and start beating everyone there with a whip?"

"Well, of course it'd be wrong," Kunkle said without hesitation.

"Well," Bolan said. "Jesus did it. The synagogue had turned into a regular flea market where the money changers were ripping everybody off. Does it seem wrong now?"

"No," Kunkle said, his eyebrows furrowing deeply.

"Why not?" the soldier persisted.

Bolan could almost see a switch click in Kunkle's head. "Well, Jesus wasn't doing it for his own personal gain, I guess," the man said slowly. "He was doing it for the good of the people, and to glorify God."

"That's exactly what we're doing, Kunkle," Bolan said. "Stealing the Jets collection is a means to a higher end."

"You're saying there's a time to fight fire with fire," the detective said.

"Exactly. We're stealing from a thief who probably stole at least part of his collection himself. Even if he paid for it, he used money he'd obtained through murders, prostitution, and a variety of other illegal and immoral means. You understand?"

Kunkle nodded slowly.

Bolan continued to stare into the man's eyes. "Then there's one more thing you need to prepare yourself for," he said. "We're extremely likely to be discovered inside Bill Dill's house tonight. And if that happens, we're either going to have to kill men or let them kill us." He stopped speaking to let the reality of the situation sink in for the detective.

"You did just fine during the gunfight at the boat dock," he finally said, "but I need to make sure you haven't been second-guessing yourself in regards to killing bad guys since then. Have you? Or are you prepared to shoot more men tonight?"

"Like you just said," Kunkle told Bolan. "I did it at the boat dock."

"That's not what I'm asking you," the soldier said. "Except for that one incident—which happened so fast you acted out of instinct—that's the only gunfight you've been in since the revival you went to. And the ones you were in before that—you were operating in a state of mind where you didn't care about your fellow man. That made it easy. But now you tell me you've had this religious awakening. And you've had plenty of time to think about the boatman, Jackson and Westbrook, back in the swamp. So are you going to be able to cover my back or am I better off leaving you here in this room?"

"If we have to shoot tonight I can do it," Kunkle said, his eyes glued to Bolan's. "I didn't like shooting the men at the boat dock, but it had to be done. It was self-defense. Us or them." He closed his eyes for a moment, then opened them again. "I believe God expects us to protect the lives he gives us. And I think he expects those of us who are able—like you and me—to protect the lives of weaker men and women who can't do it on their own."

The Executioner nodded. It was exactly what he'd hoped to hear. "Then let's get back to business," he said, pointing to the drawing of the house again. "Dill very well may have bodyguards who spend the night inside his house. McFarley thinks he does. So, like I said, we'll have to deal with them if they see us. And the man is bound to have a high-tech security system."

"Can you defeat the system?" Kunkle asked.

"Given enough time to study the setup, yeah," Bolan said. "But we don't have that much time."

"Well, don't look at me," Kunkle said. "I'm no good with that techno-geek stuff at all."

The soldier laughed softly. "Actually, I think you've got a better chance of circling the alarm system than I do," he said. "You just don't know it yet."

Then, with Kunkle's face a mask of confusion, Bolan pulled out his cell phone and handed it to the detective.

11

The meeting took place at the Dixie Diner, two blocks south of the Hotel Lafitte on a small side street. Bolan didn't think anyone had followed him to the hotel, or was watching it, but there was still no point in taking the chance of being spotted with a man who was supposed to be dead. At least not when he didn't have to.

"Give me a five minute head start," he told Kunkle as he stood by the door to the hallway. "You say the guy's name is Foreman?"

"Ernie Foreman." Kunkle nodded. He glanced at his watch. "He should be there by now, and he'll probably be in uniform. If not, just take a seat somewhere and I'll find him when I get there."

Bolan nodded, twisted the doorknob and left the room.

The sidewalk was crowded as Bolan left the hotel through the front entrance, but his eyes skirted every face he walked past, looking for any sign of interest on the part of the other pedestrians. Twice, at the corners, he stopped as if he was trying to decide which way to go, and used the ploy as an excuse to look behind him.

It was impossible to be sure. But he didn't think anyone

was tailing him either on foot or in any of the automobiles that passed in the street.

The diner's neon sign had just lit up when Bolan crossed the street and hurried toward it. A moment later, the street-lights up and down the block flickered on, then off, then on again as dusk turned into nighttime. Bolan stared at the words painted on the glass front of the café, noting that their specialty was something called the Big Easy Cheeseburger. But like most every other restaurant in the city, they also had po'boy sandwiches and fresh oysters on the half shell.

Bolan spotted the uniform in one of the back booths the second he stepped inside. A sign next to the cash register asked him to Please Wait to Be Seated. He had barely halted when an attractive waitress wearing a short white skirt and matching blouse hurried up to him and said, "Just one?"

"I'm meeting a couple of friends," Bolan replied. "And I think I see one of them in the back, there."

The young woman looked up at him and batted her eye-lashes. A wide and sexy smile curled the corners of her lips as she made no pretence of looking Bolan up and down. "Well," she almost purred in a low but strong Cajun accent, "if you ever need any other friends, my name's Yvonne."

Bolan smiled back at her. "I'll keep that in mind," he said as he started toward the back of the café.

Kunkle had described Ernie Foreman as a somewhat over-weight, slovenly officer who was assigned to silent alarm alert duty for the NOPD. What that entailed was essentially answering the phone when an alarm in someone's house or place of business went off and the owners or proprietors didn't enter the code to turn it off within the allotted "grace period." Which was usually thirty seconds to one minute. When that happened, the security company tried calling the site. If no one answered the phone, or whoever answered couldn't give them the right code, they called the police.

So it was here where Ernie Foreman entered Bolan's plan.

As he drew near the booth, Bolan saw that Kunkle's description of Foreman as *somewhat* overweight and slovenly had been a vast understatement. The man was sitting, but he didn't look as if he was over 5'6" tall. And he had to tip the scales at over three hundred pounds. His uniform, both pants and shirt, were spotted with food stains and gray ashes, and a half-smoked cigar stuck out of the top of one of the chest pockets of his uniform blouse.

The sight made Bolan recall one other fact which Kunkle had brought to his attention: the man's nickname was Dirty Ernie, and it had nothing to do with Clint Eastwood or the *Dirty Harry* movies.

Between the stains, Bolan saw the name tag opposite his badge. It read Foreman. So Bolan sat down across from him.

Foreman looked up, his tiny little eyes set deeply in his fleshy face, and stared at Bolan with a ferretlike gaze. He was in the middle of a huge bite of a po'boy and he didn't bother to swallow before saying, "Where's Kunkle?"

"He's on his way," Bolan said. "He should be here in a minute or two."

Foreman nodded, and Bolan watched a huge lump of half-chewed sandwich go down his throat, causing the Adam's apple, which had previously been hidden by fat, to finally peek into sight. In his mind, Bolan couldn't help picturing a boa constrictor swallowing a small pig. Before speaking again, Foreman opened his mouth wider than Bolan would have ever thought possible, stuffed at least a quarter of the long sandwich inside, and bit it off like one of the hungry alligators that had been in the swamps during the airboat ride.

The loud smacking sound Foreman had exhibited on the previous bite returned.

The same dark-haired, dark-eyed Cajun waitress who had greeted Bolan earlier—Yvonne—suddenly appeared at the table. She gave Foreman a quick disgusted glance, then turned to Bolan. "Can I give you something?" she asked.

Then, with horribly fake exaggeration, she corrected herself. "Sorry. I meant can I *get* you something?"

"How about a cup of coffee and one of your Big Easy burgers?" Bolan said.

Yvonne smiled again, then turned and wriggled her hips back and forth as she walked away.

Foreman still had food in his mouth and covering half of his face as he watched the woman walk away. "I'm gonna get me some of that one of these days," he said with half-chewed lettuce, cold cuts and yellow mustard spilling out of his mouth onto the table.

Bolan kept a straight face as he said, "I have absolutely no doubt you'll be successful."

Before any more could be said, Bolan heard the door open at the front of the café and Kunkle walked in. He saw Bolan and Foreman as quickly as the Executioner had spotted the uniformed officer, and walked directly to the table.

"Kunkle, I almost didn't recognize you," Ernie said, in reference to Kunkle's recent makeover.

"Hey, Ernie," he said, simply nodding as he took a seat across from the man next to Bolan. "I see you two have already met."

"Not officially," Foreman said. He had finished the po'boy and was currently cramming French fries into his face.

"Well, then," Kunkle said. "Ernie Foreman, meet Matt Cooper."

Foreman extended a big padded paw across the table. It was streaked with bright red ketchup, and Bolan said, "There's no need for formalities."

The filthy hand was more than happy to retract itself and dig back into the French fries.

"Let's get right to the point," Bolan said, glancing at Kunkle. Then, turning back to the slovenly figure across from him, he said, "Kunkle will explain it to you, but basically, what we need is your help. And we're willing to pay for it."

At the sound of the word "pay" the uniform cop's attention suddenly turned from his meal to Bolan and Kunkle.

The detective cleared his throat. Then, in an almost whispered voice, he said, "You're working tonight, right, Ernie?"

Foreman nodded. He was still eating his French fries but at a slower and less vulgar rate than before. "Graveyard," he said, and a piece of brown and white potato dribbled out of his mouth onto his uniform. "Eleven to seven shift."

"That's perfect," Kunkle said. "Here's what's going to happen. Somewhere around midnight, you're going to get a call from Bill Dill's security system contractor. We need you to squash it and put it down as a false alarm. Don't dispatch any officers to the house."

Foreman had finally finished his French fries and glanced in the direction of the waitress. She was in the process of loading Bolan's order onto a tray in the window that led to the kitchen.

"You've got to be kidding," Foreman said. "Bill Dill?"

A second later Yvonne was setting the burger and a cup of coffee in front of Bolan. She still had her eyes on Bolan, but she smiled and said to Kunkle, "What can I get you?"

"Same as my friend's having will do," Kunkle told her.

"And bring me some chocolate pie," Foreman chimed in. "Two pieces. No, wait. Make it one piece of chocolate, the other pecan."

Yvonne rolled her eyes in revulsion at the order, glanced back seductively at Bolan, then turned and strutted away again.

"So," Foreman said, his mouth finally empty. "You want me to kill the call on Bill Dill's house. Well, that's easy enough. But what am I supposed to do if he calls in later? Or comes in tomorrow wondering and asking questions as to why no officers showed up?"

Kunkle looked at the man with stone-cold eyes. "Ernie," he said, "we're talking about Bill Dill here. He's not your average, hardworking, tax-paying Joe Blow citizen. Do you really think he's going to want cops traipsing through his house to investigate what's going to be a relatively minor burglary?" He paused a second, then glanced at Bolan.

Bolan reached into an inside pocket of his jacket and pulled out a plain white envelope, shoving it across the table to Foreman. "There are five hundred-dollar bills inside," he said in a voice so low it was almost imperceptible. "You can count them if you'd like to."

Foreman grabbed the white envelope and stuffed it into his breast pocket next to the half-smoked cigar. "Are you crazy?" he said. "You're supposed to hand me that kind of thing *under* the table."

"Sorry," Bolan said, "but it's been my experience here in New Orleans that everything's pretty much out in the open."

Yvonne returned with another cheeseburger and coffee for Kunkle, and two pieces of pie for Foreman. Bolan was halfway surprised when the man across from him didn't just shove his face into the pie plates like a hog at the feeding trough. But Foreman's mind was on money at the moment, and he said, "I'm taking a chance doing this. I think another five hundred is called for, don't you? Let's make it an even grand. One large."

Bolan had expected this and he leaned into the table, pulling his jacket open to reveal another white envelope sticking up out of the inner pocket. "There's five more in here," he said as he closed his coat and sat back again. "But like I said, you don't get it until tomorrow. After the job's done and we're sure you did your part."

Foreman didn't like waiting, but he nodded in agreement.

Bolan and Kunkle began to eat their burgers and Foreman started in on his pie. The cop had downed the piece of chocolate pie before the other two men could swallow their first bite of burger. And before they took their second bite, the pecan pie was gone as well.

Foreman wedged himself out of the booth and stood up. His lips and one cheek were smeared with chocolate. "I'll expect to hear from you tomorrow," he said to Bolan and Kunkle. Then, with a final glance toward Yvonne—who was bent over at another booth, wiping it off with a damp cloth—he waddled out of the café.

"There you have it, Cooper," Kunkle said, shaking his head in embarrassment. "New Orleans finest."

"There's still more good cops than bad," Bolan said.

"I hope so," Kunkle said. "And I'm praying that I can become one of them."

12

The first line of defense they encountered was the wrought-iron fence that surrounded Bill Dill's mansion. It wasn't hard to climb over, but the pair of barking and growling Doberman pinschers who came sprinting toward them with death in their eyes were another matter.

Bolan drew the tranquilizer pistol from an unzipped pocket in his blacksuit and fired twice. The *pfffffftt* sound coming from the gun was similar to the whisper that came from the sound-suppressed Beretta 93-R. Both dogs stopped in their tracks. They whined for a moment, then lay down and closed their eyes.

"How long will they be out?" Kunkle whispered to Bolan.

"Two hours. Maybe three."

"We should be long gone by then," Kunkle said.

"One way or another," Bolan whispered. Crouching slightly, he began jogging past the dogs toward a swimming pool behind the house.

Kunkle ran next to him. "What's that supposed to mean?" the detective asked.

As the two men continued to cross the meticulously manicured lawn toward the swimming pool, Bolan answered. "It means that even though we've got a drawing of the house, and Ernie Foreman plans to ignore the alarm when it goes off, there are always surprises." He veered to his left, circumnavigating the chain-link fence around the swimming pool and cabana house, and headed toward a rear porch they had seen on the drawing.

Bolan glanced toward Kunkle. The man wore one of Bolan's extra blacksuits—a skintight, stretchy battle ensemble with multiple pockets. The suit was slightly large on the smaller man, but the elastic throughout the garment helped the fit. Around his waist, Kunkle had fastened the old Sam Browne belt from his uniformed days, which held both his 9 mm SIG-Sauer and his backup NAA .380 auto along with magazines for both weapons.

Bolan, of course, wore his .44 Magnum Desert Eagle on a black nylon web belt. The extra magazine carrier—also of ballistic nylon—rode opposite the big pistol. The 9 mm Beretta 93-R, complete with sound suppressor, was housed as usual in his shoulder rig. And an extra pair of 20-round magazines helped balance the machine pistol's weight under his right arm.

But it was to his most silent of all weapons that Bolan turned to first as soon as he and Kunkle had reached the screened-in porch. The door was locked. So Bolan drew the huge Cold Steel Espada from his blacksuit, snagging the opener on the corner of its pocket and letting it click open on its own. The click as the blade locked into place went unnoticed—the night sounds of the birds in the trees and the crickets hidden in the darkness masking the noise.

Seeing no signs that this door was wired to the alarm system, Bolan thrust the point of the big folder's blade through the screen just above the knob. He cut downward. Then, reaching inside, his hand found the simple "hook and eye" lock and lifted it.

A moment later, Kunkle had been ushered inside and the Executioner quietly closed the door behind them.

Bolan pulled the small ASP laser flashlight from another blacksuit pocket and flashed it on briefly. In the center of the back porch was an iron table and chairs, all painted white. The wall against the house had come from the same white brick with which the house itself had been built, and a floor-to-ceiling fireplace sat in the center.

Bolan risked another quick beam of light at the fireplace. It was filled with dried leaves and other debris, and didn't look as if it had been used in years.

The Executioner turned his attention to the first of the two doors leading into the house from the porch. It was a normal-looking door, and another quick shot of laser light through the windows in the upper half told Bolan it was a long thin room, totally glassed in on the outside of the house, and filled with potted plants and flowers.

The conservatory, just as the drawing had listed it.

Bolan faced a Dutch door, next to the fireplace. It was windowless, heavy, and of ancient timber that looked almost medieval in the dim lighting. The lock in the bottom half of the door was of a year gone by as well, and when he shone his flashlight through the hole he could see that an archaic, skeleton-type key was shoved into it on the inside.

Bolan paused, thinking. According to the blueprints, the room to which this door led was called the family room, and it was directly below the study upstairs where he and Kunkle expected to find the bulk of Dill's New York Jets collection. He pulled a set of lock picks from his blacksuit, unzipped it, then turned toward Kunkle who was directly behind him. "Get ready," Bolan said. "As soon as the door swings open, the alarm is going to go off. We've got to get inside and find a place to hide before Dill—or one of his employees pulling night guard duty—comes to check things out."

"What if they're already in the family room?" Kunkle asked.

"Then we're screwed as far as clandestine entry goes," Bolan said. "I'd suggest you start shooting."

Even in the dim light, Bolan could see that Kunkle was slightly uncomfortable. "Are we sure they aren't legitimate hired security guards?" he whispered.

Bolan knew that Kunkle's newfound religious convictions were giving him trouble again, and it would take time for them to balance. But he felt it was his duty to straighten out the NOPD cop until he leveled off as to "right and wrong" on his own. "Greg," he said quietly, "does it make much sense for a man who has professional gunmen on his payroll to hire rent-a-cops to protect him at night?"

Kunkle waited a moment, then nodded.

Bolan used one of his picks to shove the key back out of the door. Through the thick wood, he faintly heard it land on the floor with a small ringing sound. That meant a wooden floor instead of carpet. And while he had heard the sound, he doubted anyone not actually in the room could have heard it.

Just to be safe, he waited a full minute before reinserting his picks. When he heard nothing further, he took it as a good sign that not only had no one heard the sound but that no one was in the family room as Kunkle had feared.

Picking the lock took less than thirty seconds.

Bolan wrapped a big hand around the doorknob, then looked back over his shoulder. "As soon as I push the door open," he whispered, "the alarm is going to go off. You go first. Find the best place you can to hide and stay still until you hear from me again. You ready?"

"As ready as I'm gonna get," the detective said.

Bolan twisted the knob, pushed on the bottom half of the split door, then moved to the side so Kunkle could crab-walk through. A low buzz began sounding throughout the mansion, and then a second later the buzz was replaced by a loud, bone-chilling siren that practically shook the whole house.

The Executioner crawled in through the opening and grabbed the key off the floor.

The immediate alarm had not surprised Bolan. During the day, there was probably a thirty to forty-five second delay from the first breach to the full blown alert siren. During that time, the low buzzer he had heard first would sound, telling the Dill family and guards that they needed to make their way to the control box and enter the pass number. But at night, this grace time was shortened to almost nothing.

Bolan turned back to the Dutch door, closed it, then jabbed the key back in the lock. In his peripheral vision, he had seen Kunkle dive behind a huge couch against the opposite wall. He risked the flashlight long enough to run the light over a large-screen television, an elaborate stereo system, two rocking chairs and various other sofas and padded seats. To his right, just inside the closed door that led to the conservatory, he saw a built-in bar.

Bolan killed the light, leaving the room almost pitch black. Moving quickly but quietly to the bar, he swung open a door in the counter, then pulled it back closed as he dropped to a squatting position. The Beretta 93-R danced out of its holster into his hand as if on its own accord, and he glanced at the numerous bottles of whiskey, vodka, gin and other spirits on the shelf. To his right was an antique Coca-Cola icebox, and to its side was a sink.

The racket of the alarm was still in his ears as Bolan settled in to wait for the inevitable. Sooner or later, Dill would turn it off, but the alarm itself would have already generated a call to the police. That's where Kunkle's "pie-eating" dispatcher, Dirty Ernie Foreman, would come in.

As he sat back on his heels, Bolan heard the alarm suddenly cease. The search would shortly begin. And if whoever came to this family room conducted anything more than a cursory check, he and Kunkle would be discovered.

And the shooting would begin.

Bolan didn't like that idea. Dill and his men might deserve death for the deeds they'd done, but according to McFarley, the man had a wife and two daughters. They *didn't* deserve such a fate. While Bolan had the confidence that if all hell broke loose he'd control his own fire and keep from harming the innocent females, he wasn't so sure about Kunkle or Dill, or Dill's bodyguards.

Angling the Beretta slightly upward, Bolan glanced at the luminous hands on his watch. And waited.

Two minutes later, the door leading into the conservatory opened and the overhead light switched on. Bolan huddled lower, the 93-R still angled toward the height at which a man's head would be if he looked over the bar. He was surprised to find the fumes of bourbon infiltrating his nostrils, and his first impulse was to glance at the bottles in front of him to see if one had cracked. Then he realized that the smell came from outside the bar.

Which had to mean it was the breath of whoever had opened the door.

Was it Dill? Or one of his men? Not that it mattered much. Either party would be armed and ready to shoot an intruder.

Bolan heard the man on the other side of the bar take several steps on the hardwood floor, then stop. From where he was, Bolan could see the top of the door. A few seconds later, he heard footsteps again and caught a brief glance of the top of a head exiting the room.

"Nothin' in here, Frank," came a voice as the light was switched off and the door closed again. "Must have been the wind shaking the windows again."

That simple statement told Bolan several things. First, it wasn't likely to have been Dill who had performed the cursory search of the family room. And the searcher had called to a man still outside the room. That meant at least two bodyguards—likely more—were inside the house, men whom he and Kunkle would have to slip past.

Or kill.

The second thing Bolan learned came from the last words out of the bodyguard's mouth. "Must have been the wind shaking the windows again." From where he still sat, Bolan could see the tiny green lights near the ceiling. The house was equipped with both sound and movement sensors aimed at the windows and doors. And such sensors sometimes went off if a strong wind shook the glass panes hard enough.

Last but not least was a partial guess on Bolan's part. The tone of the man's voice insinuated that the family room was the last room the guards had searched. They were likely to be headed back toward wherever they were stationed.

But Bolan had not survived his innumerable battles by taking unnecessary chances. So he waited a good fifteen minutes more before standing up in the darkness. Then, slowly and quietly, he swung the bar door back open, aimed his flashlight toward the wall above the large couch and flashed it on and off three times.

Kunkle stood up slowly, his SIG-Sauer in his hand. "That was close," he whispered.

Bolan nodded.

"Could you see who it was who came in?" the detective asked.

Bolan shook his head. "Only caught a glance. But I don't think it was Dill."

"Even if it wasn't," Kunkle said, "we'd better wait a while for him to get back to sleep. You can be sure that the alarm at least woke him up."

"And don't forget that there are at least two guards on duty. The one who came in here reeked of booze."

Kunkle nodded. "I could smell him from behind the couch."

The soldier didn't bother commenting further.

Fifteen minutes went by, then a half hour, then an hour. Finally, Bolan whispered, "Let's do it." But before he started toward the rustic door leading to the conservatory, he added, "Keep in mind that bodyguards are likely to pop up at any time." He had drawn the Beretta 93-R with the sound suppressor threaded onto the barrel. "I want everything quiet for as long as we can pull it off." He glanced at the SIG-Sauer in Kunkle's hand "So unless it's absolutely life or death, let me handle any surprises with this whisperer."

Kunkle nodded, and the two men started toward the door. And whatever waited behind it.

13

In the moonlight coming in through the glass wall of the conservatory, Bolan could see that the floor was made of unusual mosaic tile. No two pieces were the same size or shape, and the hues ran the spectrum of the color chart. Dozens, if not hundreds, of plants were potted in vases along the glass wall, and they varied as widely in size, shape and color as the tile on the floor.

The Beretta held down at his side, Bolan crept slowly toward a set of double doors to his left, halfway through the long thin conservatory. From the floor plan drawing he kept folded in a pocket, Bolan knew these doors led into the house's large formal living room. Peering slowly around the corner of the open doors, he saw a baby grand piano to his left. Two love seats faced each other and another large couch—this one in leather—took up the right-hand wall. Farther into the huge room, just inside the front windows of the house, was another pair of facing love seats.

The room had the feel of one that was rarely used.

Looking beyond the living room to his right, Bolan could see that light burned in what appeared to be the foyer. According to the drawing, the main staircase started just out of sight, behind the opposite wall. A back staircase could be accessed if he walked down the conservatory, past a downstairs bathroom and through the kitchen. But the kitchen was a likely place for the guards to congregate during the night, and since Bolan knew there were at least two inside the house, he didn't want to risk gunfire breaking out while they were still downstairs.

The soldier knew for certain that there were at least two guards on duty, but more importantly, his gut told him there would be more. So the front staircase was the one he needed to take. He doubted that more than one man would be there.

As he pulled back around the corner, Bolan saw a glimmer of movement in front of the stairs. It came almost at lightning speed, and as best he could make out it was the shoulder of a white shirt.

The glimmer of white told Bolan his instincts had been correct. There *was* at least one man at the foot of the steps, but that was the way he needed to go.

"Stick your gun back in the holster," Bolan whispered to Kunkle. "And follow me. Quietly." He turned the corner off the mosaic tile and stepped onto the thick carpeting of the living room.

Bolan walked past the piano and moved into the shadows of the wall to his left. Slowly and silently, he slid his feet across the carpet to get an angle of fire into the foyer. After only a few short shuffling steps, a strange smacking sound met his ears. Then the white shirt he had seen moments earlier came into view.

One of Dill's night guards was sitting on the front steps. A sport coat was folded sloppily on the stair next to him, and over his white shirt Bolan could see a vertical shoulder holster that carried some sort of automatic pistol.

The smacking sound came from the apple the man was munching on.

The Executioner raised the sound-suppressed Beretta to eye level then fired from the shadows. The 93-R coughed out a single 9 mm hollowpoint round that drilled through the center of the guard's chest just as he took another bite of the apple. The half-eaten piece of fruit fell to the step beneath which the man sat and rolled up against the front door of the house. The man fell backward, sprawled out dead on the steps.

Bolan waved for Kunkle to follow him again as he crossed the darkened room into the lighted foyer. Temporarily holstering the Beretta, he grabbed one of the bodyguard's arms. Without being told to, Kunkle grabbed the other and they dragged the corpse back into the shadows of the living room, dropping him out of sight behind one of the love seats.

Bolan led the way again, entering the foyer and walking backwards up the steps, the Beretta 93-R held above his head. He had gone less than three steps when he saw another guard just outside Bill Dill's bedroom.

And at the same time he saw the guard, the guard saw him.

The man drew a four-inch Smith & Wesson Model 629 from his hip holster. But before he could fire and awaken the house, Bolan put a double-tap of quiet 9 mm rounds into his chest. The man toppled forward against the railing that surrounded the staircase on the upper level, then fell over it.

With the speed of a jungle cat, Bolan holstered his weapon and reached up, catching the falling man in his arms and cushioning the sound as his body hit the steps. Without words, the soldier handed his burden to Kunkle, who nodded and then dragged the man out of sight into the living room with his partner.

Bolan took two more steps up the staircase, then stopped. From where he was, he could see the door to Dill's bedroom as well as one of the girl's rooms directly across from it. According to the drawing, a long hallway led from the two rooms. But the door to it was closed. Bolan also knew from the drawing that this hall led to two more bedrooms—one of them over the garage—and between them, the back staircase.

The soldier paused, thinking. He suspected there had to be at least one more guard in charge of that wing of the house. The closed door told him whoever, and however many, they were, had not been alerted to what was going on in the front. So, moving slightly faster, Bolan backed on up the steps to the second floor.

Kunkle still had his SIG-Sauer in its holster as he reappeared and followed.

The light in the upstairs area was on, but Bolan turned it off as soon as he reached the switch. He seriously doubted that Dill would want a guard inside his and his wife's bedroom. Opening the door and letting the outside illumination in might well awaken one or both of them. And while the Executioner had no qualms about killing Dill if need be, he had no intention of harming his wife.

Bolan could barely hear Kunkle's feet as the man climbed the steps behind him. He moved next to the darkened bedroom door and pressed an ear to the small crack between the door and the frame. Inside, he could hear two different snores. One was loud and throaty. The other was more quiet and peaceful.

Both Dill and his wife were asleep, and the loud snore led Bolan to believe it was a deep sleep. The other snore he wasn't so sure about.

The creak the bedroom door made when he opened it was negligible. But to Bolan, it sounded like a giant timber being felled. He stopped with the door cracked and continued listening. But the snores didn't change.

With the door open just enough to squeeze through, Bolan entered the bedroom. In a dim light that came through the window facing the front of the house, he stared at the two sleeping forms on the bed. Kunkle left the door where it was as he slipped through sideways, and then Bolan began leading the way past the bed into what the crude drawing promised was a short hallway from the bedroom, past Dill's private clothes closet, and into the study where the New York Jets collection was kept.

The bedroom was carpeted like the hallway. But the hall, closet and study had the same hardwood floor that he had found in the family room. There was no way to keep it from creaking as Bolan and Kunkle moved slowly on.

As soon as Kunkle had stepped out of the bedroom to the hall, Bolan closed the door behind him as quietly as possible. It still creaked. But Bolan heard no signs of Dill or his wife awakening. The house was elegant but old, and probably settled fairly noisily every night. Which meant the two figures sleeping in the bed were used to such noises.

With the door to the bedroom closed again, Bolan turned on the hall light. He crept past the huge walk-in closet into the study, switching the overhead light on in this room as well. The walls were lined with bookshelves. A huge desk faced him and was cluttered with papers. Several other pieces of furniture were scattered around the room, and two small closets, angling down with the contour of the house's roof, were just to his right.

Bolan saw everything one might expect to see in the home office of a criminal: computer, printer, fax and adding machines. Even a money counter. But he saw absolutely nothing green or pertaining to the New York Jets.

Bolan turned toward Kunkle and saw the confusion on the detective's face as well. The drawing of the house had been accurate so far, but McFarley's belief that the Jets collection was kept in the study had been wrong.

Slowly and silently, Bolan lifted the latches to both closets. One was packed with old clothing and blankets. The other was stuffed with empty suitcases. Bolan turned to Kunkle again. "Let's check his clothes closet," he whispered.

The detective nodded.

Bolan led the way back into the short hallway, then turned to his right and switched on the closet light. To his left hung dozens of suits, slacks and sport coats. To his right was a built-in bureau and mirror.

But again, he saw nothing green.

Bolan took two more steps deeper into the closet to allow Kunkle to enter. Just past the clothing was a chair, and the other side of the closet was made of drawers that connected to the bureau. Hanging from the rear wall on a hanger was a gray sweatshirt. But not even the sweatshirt said anything about the New York Jets.

Bolan held up a hand, which told Kunkle to stop, and the detective froze in his tracks. The soldier handed the man his Beretta, then opened the top drawer as quietly as possible. In the corner of his eye, he could see that Kunkle was somewhat surprised that he'd been trusted with the machine pistol. But in Bolan's eyes the man had proved that a change really had taken place in his heart.

Bolan found nothing but folded clothing in the top drawer. Or in any of the drawers beneath it.

Bolan glanced at the sweatshirt hanging on the wall once more, then turned away. But just as quickly, he turned back. Something had caught his attention. What was it? He stared at the shirt again, concentrating, and suddenly saw what had struck his subconscious mind.

It wasn't the shirt itself. It was the crack in the wood paneling of which the closet walls were constructed. Running from the ceiling to the floor, behind the hanging sweatshirt, the crack was at least twice as large as the spaces between the other panels on the wall.

Bolan reached out and took the hanger off the wall, laying the sweatshirt down on the chair. Reaching out, he stuck his fingers into the crack and it opened slightly wider.

Staring down at the floor, Bolan saw that the panel had moved out toward his feet an inch or so. And a second later, he had slid the piece of wall out and leaned it against the drawers.

Bolan had seen no signs of green before, but in this hidden room he saw nothing *but* green. There seemed to be no apparent order to the chaos. Two tables and four chairs were piled high with New York Jets programs, autographed papers, news clippings, T-shirts, jerseys and bobble-head dolls. On the walls were pennants and autographed photographs, as well as several green jerseys, including one number 12, framed under glass and signed by Joe Namath.

Behind him, Bolan heard Kunkle whisper, "I think we've struck gold."

"Or green," Bolan replied in a quiet voice. "Go back and get the two biggest suitcases you can find in that study closet," he whispered. "We'll take all of this stuff we can carry."

Kunkle nodded and turned back away.

Bolan moved on into the room. He knew that McFarley didn't want the Jets collection for himself. He just didn't want Dill to have it, and he wanted Dill to know who was behind the theft. So it wasn't particularly important that he get the more fragile items—like the bobble-head dolls and other breakable memorabilia out in one piece—just that they get them out.

Kunkle returned a few seconds later with two huge, soft-sided suitcases. The two night prowlers began, swiftly but silently, filling the luggage with the souvenirs. Bolan thought while he packed. They weren't out of the woods quite yet. On their way out they had to slip past the sleeping gangster and his wife again, then dodge, or kill, any remaining bodyguards on the premises. And this all had to be done while carrying suitcases at least twice the normal size, which would easily weigh over a hundred pounds apiece when packed.

Not to mention making good their escape without any harm being done to Dill's wife or daughters.

When they had finally stuffed everything they could into the suitcases, Bolan said, "Okay. Let's go. But keep in mind that just jiggling these things as we carry them is going to make extra noise. So if it comes down to it, we leave this stuff behind and get out without the women getting hurt. Understand?"

"I understand," Kunkle whispered back.

Bolan led the way back out of the hidden room, let Kunkle pass by him into the closet again, then replaced the removable panel. He pulled up on the suitcase, then let it slide to the end of his fingers, hearing a soft clinking and clanking of the contents. Repeating the procedure twice more, he let the souvenirs settle in the hope that they would make less noise as they left the house.

Kunkle caught on to what he was doing, understood why and copied the procedure with his own bag.

Bolan killed the closet and hall lights, then slowly opened the door to the bedroom. The snoring continued just as it had, but as he stepped back onto the carpet and moved past the bed, he was surprised to notice for the first time that the loud snoring came from Mrs. Dill and that it was McFarley's nemesis who snored softly.

The old saying "No rest for the wicked" crossed Bolan's mind. But experience had taught him that it was an adage upon which you could never rely. Some men seemed to be born without a conscience, and they could cut the throat of an innocent baby and then go to sleep like one five minutes later.

The two intruders were halfway to the door leading out of the bedroom when Dill suddenly sat upright in bed. In the streetlight that shone though the window, Bolan could see that there was a gun aimed at him in the shadows.

"Frank? Jeff?" the sleepy voice said. "I told you… Wait, you're not—"

And that was as far as Dill got. They were his dying words just before a sound-suppressed 9 mm bullet caught him squarely on the bridge of his nose.

But the words were not the criminal's last sound. That

came from the pistol in his hand, and whatever caliber it was, Bolan knew it was loud enough to be heard throughout the mansion.

The time for stealth was suddenly over.

And the time for open battle had begun.

14

Dill's wife had been awakened by the explosion. She sat up in bed and screamed at the top of her lungs. The shriek was even more piercing than Dill's pistol round had been.

Bolan turned toward Kunkle, knowing there was no sense in whispering anymore. As the sounds of the gunshot and Mrs. Dill's scream died down around them, he spoke in a loud, commanding voice. "We've got to get this fight away from the wife and girls. That includes the bedroom right across from us." Without another word, he threw open the door and stepped outside.

One of Dill's hired killers had just come into the area with the railing around the stairs. In his hand was a sawed-off double-barreled shotgun. The open door to the long hallway told Bolan that was the area of the house from which he'd come.

The man was directly in front of the door to whichever of the daughters occupied the bedroom across from Dill and his wife. And Bolan had no idea how the furniture was arranged inside the room behind the barrier. But what he did know was that when using 9 mm ammo—even the RBCD total fragmentation rounds he had in the Beretta—there was always the chance that a missed round would penetrate the door. If it did, it might also take out the girl in bed behind it.

So without thinking, Bolan instinctively dropped to one knee, angling the Beretta upward at the man's head. Without further hesitation, he fired another soft-sounding round that took the goon's right eye. As well as his life.

Bolan jumped back to his feet. He had set the suitcase down beside him when he knelt, and he grabbed the handle again. It was also time to quit using the Beretta. Silence was no longer in his favor, and the more pandemonium and confusion he could create the better.

Drawing the huge .44 Magnum Desert Eagle from his web belt, Bolan rounded the railing. In doing so, he had to pass the open hallway to the other end of the house. And as he did, a 3-round burst of what sounded like M-16 fire flew by him, one round passing so close to his ear that he felt the breeze it generated.

He could have gone on. But since the man—or *men*—down the hallway knew that there was one intruder, they'd guess there might be more. Which meant that Kunkle was likely to catch multiple rounds when he crossed the open door. So, pressing his back against the wall just out of sight, Bolan shifted the big .44 to his left hand and held the awkward suitcase in his right. He looked at Kunkle, who was still just a step out of Dill's bedroom, and held up a hand, signaling for the detective to wait. Then dropping to one knee again, he peered around the corner and saw a shadowy form holding an assault rifle still standing in the hall. Pulling back for a moment, the soldier let another 3-round burst fly past him, then leaned out with the Desert Eagle and put a semi-jacketed hollowpoint bullet into the middle of the rifleman's chest.

Lugging his suitcase in one hand, Kunkle joined him on the other side of the hall door.

Bolan led the way down the steps, the Desert Eagle in one

hand, the suitcase filled with Jets memorabilia in the other. He had seen Kunkle draw his SIG-Sauer when he'd traded the Beretta for the Desert Eagle, and he realized he would at least have some sort of backup as he fought his way out of the house. Bolan had no idea how many guards were still on two feet inside the mansion, so he would have to deal with them as he came to them.

And he came to another pair almost immediately.

Bolan was barely halfway down the front stairs again when one gunner appeared from out of the living room. At the same time, another man came from the other side. From the drawing of the house, Bolan knew the man had to have emerged from the formal dining room with its swing door that led to the kitchen. Not that it mattered much. Regardless of where he had come from, he was *there* at this moment. And armed.

The first .44 Magnum round exploded into the head of the man from the living room as he tried to bring his Colt Government Model .45 auto into play. He stood still for a moment, half his head gone and the other half a mass of brain tissue, blood and skull fragments. As he finally collapsed, Bolan turned the big gun on the man who had come from the dining room. As he fired a second shot into the gunman's heart, he saw a mist of blood shoot out of the man's front while bloody tissue and spinal parts blew out the back.

Behind him, almost deafening in his ear, he heard Kunkle's 9 mm pistol erupt and put two more rounds into the body.

Bolan vaulted down the steps, lugging the clumsy suitcase with him. When he reached the bottom, he turned to look at the doorway that led into the living room. Should he lead Kunkle back out the same way they had come? At least they knew the terrain that way.

Bolan peered into the living room and the decision was made for him when a half-dozen men with assault rifles, shotguns and pistols opened up, narrowly missing him as he jerked his head back to cover.

Bolan felt the vibrations as the rounds hit the wall in front of him. And he silently thanked the Universe that the house was old enough to have had the walls built with plaster and lathe rather than the thin plasterboard of newer homes.

Bounding past the front door and into the dining room, Bolan saw a huge dining table, matching chairs and several china cabinets. He circled the table and chairs, hearing Kunkle's footsteps right behind him. He was almost to the swing door to the kitchen when he heard another double-tap of 9 mm rounds. Looking over his shoulder, Bolan saw that another man had entered the foyer, and that Kunkle had downed him before he could lift the semiautomatic 12-gauge shotgun in his hands.

Bolan pushed the swing door open, then went in low. As he did so, a blast of three 7.62 mm rounds from an AK-47 streaked over his head. Another of Dill's guards stood next to the sink, a Russian Kalashnikov rifle in his hands, preparing to fire again.

The soldier pointed the Desert Eagle at the guard and sent a pair of .44 Magnum rounds into his chest and throat. Then, rushing toward the fallen man, he lifted the Russian rifle and checked the magazine. It felt full—except for the three rounds fired at him. That was good because Bolan found only one other magazine in the back pocket of the man's slacks. It was loaded with pointed, armor-piercing rounds.

Bolan shoved the extra magazine into one of the pockets of his blacksuit.

By this point, Kunkle had entered the kitchen and Bolan saw that the NOPD detective had appropriated the semiauto shotgun from his last victim. Not that you could call any of these house guards victims, Bolan thought. They had given up such status when they'd gone to work for a man like Dill.

They had, instead of victims, become enemy combatants.

From the plans of the house that he had studied, Bolan knew that the door to his right led past the back staircase and onto a small porch. The porch had two outside doors, one leading into the garage, the other to the outside and another small, screened-in area. With the AK-47 stock under his right arm, and the huge suitcase filled with Jets memorabilia in his left hand, he started that way.

But there was another side door to the kitchen that connected it to the hallways where the downstairs bathroom stood. As the soldier crossed the kitchen, a shaved head with a huge handlebar mustache and a Ruger automatic pistol gripped in two hands appeared, framed in the doorway. The face above the mustache looked frightened.

Bolan let the suitcase fall from his left hand to the floor. He twisted hard to get the barrel of the AK-47 around and pointed toward the man. When he did, a full-auto stream of rounds stitched the man from groin to mustache. He was dead before he hit the kitchen floor on his face.

Kunkle had picked up on the fact that the man he knew as Cooper wanted to leave the house through the kitchen exit. With the shotgun's stock under his arm—similar to the way Bolan held the Kalashnikov—and his own suitcase gripped in his left hand, he stepped out in front of the back staircase. Almost immediately, the 12-gauge semiauto shotgun erupted in two distinct roars, and another pair of Dill's henchmen came tumbling down the back steps into view.

Bolan moved on out of the kitchen, stepping over the tangled men Kunkle had just shot and stopping less than a foot behind the detective. From where he stood, he could see that yet another set of steps, next to the back stairs, led downward—undoubtedly into a basement. These steps, as well as the basement below, had not been on the drawing. But Bolan saw no sign of gunmen coming up the steps. So he stopped and pivoted, covering the kitchen once more.

Kunkle had to set his suitcase down in order to open the door to the outside, then he stepped through it. Bolan, walking backward, followed. He was almost through the door when a man with long stringy hair and a 9 mm Heckler & Koch 94 carbine appeared in the kitchen through the swing door to the dining room.

A 3-round burst from the AK-47 sent two rounds directly through the long-haired man's heart. The third round of the burst hit high from the recoil. It entered the gunner's left eye socket and sent blood, brains and broken bits of facial bone exploding out of the back of the man's head.

Bolan took the lead again, hurrying around Kunkle and pushing through the screen door to the outside of the house. They had entered the dwelling through the back. But presently they saw that a long winding drive led to a closed gate at the front of the property. Several gate guards stood ready to shoot them as soon as they got the chance. Three others had abandoned their post and were sprinting toward the house. All three carried Uzis.

And all three Uzis were aimed at Bolan and Kunkle.

The Israeli submachine guns began to sputter when the men were still thirty yards away, sending 9 mm rounds past Bolan and Kunkle like a flock of angry birds. The Executioner stopped in his tracks and steadied the AK-47, looking down the barrel through the sights. Firing one-handed, he blasted a lone 7.62 mm bullet from the old Soviet weapon. The round exploded through the lead runner's chest.

The guard dropped to the driveway, and the man running just behind him tripped over him.

Bolan pulled the trigger again, shooting the second man as he stumbled and fell. The single round caught him on the ear, ripping the flapping flesh away from the side of his head and causing him to scream. The soldier shot one-handed again, and the screaming stopped as the rifle round entered the hole where the ear had been and expanded upon contact, exploding the gate guard's head as if a stick of dynamite had gone off inside a watermelon.

Kunkle had leveled the shotgun on the third running man.

He wore a white shirt, making him an easy target in the moonlight, and a 12-gauge blast caught him in the chest.

As Bolan turned his assault rifle toward the men still at the gate, he watched the white turn black with blood.

A huge pine tree stood to the side of the driveway and Bolan dropped his suitcase momentarily as he dived, then rolled, behind it. Rifle rounds from more assault rifles followed him, kicking up dirt and grass as he rolled, then lodging in the tree trunk as he popped back to his feet behind it. Kunkle, he saw, had flattened on the ground, which made Bolan frown.

It was not a wise move on the detective's part. Even though he made a smaller target, he was still out in the open and sooner or later one or more of the rounds pounding around him would find their mark.

Bolan squinted in the moonlight, following the angle of the shots back to a man who stood partially in, partially out, of the concrete guard shack. The gate guard was wielding an M-16, and sending a steady stream of 5.56 rounds toward Kunkle.

"Move!" Bolan shouted to the detective, then pulled the trigger of his Kalashnikov again. Two more rounds pounded into the gate guard's shoulder and caused him to drop the American-made rifle. A look of shock covered his face for a second before Bolan squeezed the trigger again, and the back of the man's head disappeared.

He fell out of the guard shack onto the pavement.

Kunkle had taken Bolan's words to heart and had scrambled to his feet. He lugged the suitcase toward the tree where the Executioner hid. "Leave it!" Bolan shouted out. "We'll get it later!"

The detective dropped the suitcase and sprinted toward Bolan.

The soldier leaned out slightly from the tree trunk and sighted down the barrel again. A lone round took out the second man still at the gate, and he rolled out onto the pavement next to his friend. The third man, however, had seen what had happened to the other two. And he was safely ensconced inside the small building, covered from the waist down by concrete but looking through the glass in the top of the window.

Bolan aimed at the man's head and pulled the trigger again. His round struck the glass, then ricocheted off with a loud whine. The window was bullet-resistant, Bolan saw.

But *nothing* was completely bulletproof.

The Executioner ejected the almost-empty magazine of 7.62 mm rounds from his rifle and inserted the other magazine—the one loaded with armor-piercing rounds—into the weapon. He fired at the same spot in the window—with the same result. The round whinnied like a colt as it bounced off the glass.

But then Bolan switched the selector to full-auto. With the stock held firmly against his shoulder, he pulled the trigger back and held it, sending a dozen armor-piercing rounds cracking, then exploding the glass in the guardhouse.

The man behind the window saw his fate as soon as the glass began to crack. He dropped down behind the concrete, out of sight.

"Keep firing!" Bolan ordered Kunkle as he left the cover of the tree and sprinted toward where the third and final gate guard hid. The detective kept up a steady boom of 12-gauge fire that peppered through the broken glass and sent pellets raining down over the hidden man.

The pellets lost most of their velocity when they struck the concrete back of the guardhouse. But by falling over the man on the floor, they created just the diversion Bolan had hoped for.

Without slowing his pace, Bolan raced to the open door of the guard shack. The final guard was squatting, and looking straight at him, as he pulled the trigger of the AK-47 again and sent a half-dozen rounds into the man's body. In the end, all of the concrete and bullet-resistant glass in the world didn't help him, and the gate guard fell onto his face just as dead as the others.

Suddenly, the house and yard grew silent. It stayed that way for a moment, then a lone cricket worked up enough courage to let out a single "click."

"Grab the suitcases!" Bolan yelled back through the gate, and watched as Kunkle let his appropriated shotgun fall to the ground and grabbed the handles of both pieces of luggage. Bolan turned to cover the house behind them, but not a single round was fired as the detective jogged toward him, awkwardly lugging the New York Jets collection as he ran.

Bolan took one of the suitcases as soon as Kunkle reached him, then turned toward a Mercedes-Benz parked just outside the guardhouse. They had left the Cadillac Escalade several blocks away, on the other side of the mansion.

In the distance, Bolan could hear sirens.

Kunkle's NOPD contact—Ernie Foreman—had squashed the burglar alarm call. But the fighting on the outside of the house had definitely gotten the attention of the neighbors, and one or more of them had called the police.

Which meant Bolan and Kunkle had to get away. Fast.

Bolan dropped the AK-47 as he swung the driver's door open. He was about to slide behind the wheel when he saw movement in the backseat and whipped the Desert Eagle from his hip holster.

The barrel moved into alignment with a whimpering Doberman pinscher puppy.

The Executioner holstered the Desert Eagle again, then lifted the frightened animal from the backseat and set him down on the ground. The last he saw of the little dog was his stubby tail as he sprinted toward the house.

The keys were in the ignition, and Bolan called out to

Kunkle again. "Put the suitcases in the back and get in. Quick."

The detective did as he was told, and Bolan started the engine. A second later, they were gliding away from the house, toward the rapidly approaching black-and-white patrol car. It passed by, siren blaring and lights flashing, speeding toward Bill Dill's house.

15

Kunkle was in a confusing state of conflicting emotions. He had been in gunfights before as a New Orleans police officer, but never on a scale such as the one he had just survived.

He sat as still as a statue as he watched Cooper drive the Mercedes three blocks from Dill's house before twirling the steering wheel into a right-hand turn and heading back toward where they had parked the Cadillac Escalade. In his chest, he could feel his heart beating as if some giant was pounding a huge kettle drum beneath his sternum. He was frightened. He was euphoric. But most of all, he was just simply amazed.

He had never seen anyone—in or out of law enforcement—who could fight like the man guiding the Mercedes.

Who in the world *was* Matt Cooper? He wasn't just some normal federal agent—they had broken far too many laws for the man to have really been a Justice Department agent like he said. No bureaucrat would hang his butt out to get killed—or later prosecuted—like Cooper had just done. No, Cooper was something special. Very special. Something that the general public, and law enforcement nationwide, didn't know anything about. The only thing Kunkle was certain about was that Matt Cooper wasn't his real name.

The Mercedes turned right again and pulled to a halt along the curb just behind where they'd parked the Escalade. Kunkle could still hear the sirens, but by then they were far in the distance. The houses along this street were all darkened; far enough away from the chaos still ensuing at Dill's house that the people inside them hadn't been disturbed.

It could not have worked out any better, Kunkle realized. The gunfire outside Dill's house had alerted his neighbors who, naturally, had called 9-1-1. But their deal with Foreman to squash the call from the security company had given them the extra time they needed to gather up the Jets paraphernalia before fighting their way to safety.

Without a word, Cooper suddenly killed the Mercedes' engine and jumped out of the car. Opening the back door on the driver's side, he reached in and grabbed one of the suitcases. Kunkle, still feeling as if he was in a daze, followed the man's lead. If truth be told, he had been following Cooper's lead all night. He got out of the Mercedes, grabbed the other suitcase and lugged it toward the Cadillac. A moment later, both men were in the Escalade and driving off again.

Kunkle realized he had more or less blacked out for a few minutes. He remembered driving away from Dill's house, then suddenly they were changing vehicles. Well, he thought, he would continue to follow Cooper. Doing so had kept him alive during the biggest and most violent gunfight of his life, so he didn't have any intention of altering that procedure.

At least not until this postbattle shock or whatever it was had worn off and he was thinking straight again.

The two men had left sport coats in the front seat of the Escalade, which they slipped over their blacksuits, hiding both their weapons and the fighting suits themselves from eyes outside of the vehicle. Cooper had not spoken since they'd left the Mercedes.

When Kunkle broke the silence, he was surprised to find that his voice cracked like that of an adolescent boy. "What now?" was all he managed to get out as his heart continued to beat drumrolls in his chest.

"I'm taking you back to the hotel," Bolan said simply. "By then, I should have just about enough time to hit my apartment, take a shower and change clothes before delivering this stuff to McFarley."

Kunkle didn't want his voice to screech again so he just nodded his understanding. As they drove on, he watched Cooper out of the corner of his eye. He had never seen a man who could fight like the big guy behind the wheel of the Caddie. He appeared to be a master of any weapon that happened to find his hands, and he seemed to know exactly what an enemy was about to do before that enemy even knew it himself. They had come within a hairbreadth of getting killed at least a dozen times during the long gunfight in and out of Dill's house. And Kunkle had watched as Cooper killed several men a split second before they were about to drop the detective.

That was another thing Kunkle knew, he decided as he leaned back and tried to tune down the percussion section in his chest. He would have never survived a gun battle of this magnitude if Cooper hadn't been leading the way.

The thumping in his chest was slowly diminishing, but in its place Kunkle noted that nausea was infiltrating his stomach. He had experienced this before—right after the other gunfights he'd been in as a cop. It was not the blood and other gore making him sick. He knew that from past experience. It was the gigantic dump of adrenaline that often followed such an encounter and had no other place to go.

"Can you...pull over a minute?" the detective asked softly. He was at least pleased that his voice didn't crack again.

Bolan didn't seem surprised in the least, and he guided the Cadillac quickly toward the curb.

Kunkle opened the door, leaned out and threw up everything he'd eaten that hadn't yet descended to his intestines. He ended the incident with a half-dozen dry heaves, then closed the door and sat back against the seat again.

The nausea was gone. But he still felt as if he wanted to sprint a mile or two, or bench press four-hundred pounds, or punch a heavy bag until his arms and legs gave out in exhaustion and he collapsed on the floor.

"It'll get better," Bolan said quietly. "It just takes a little time."

Kunkle took a deep breath and let it out slowly. "How come all this isn't happening to you?" he asked.

"I'm used to it," Bolan replied, and Kunkle was half-surprised to hear no tone of reproach or sarcasm in the man's voice. Then again, when he really thought about it, it wasn't so surprising. It seemed Cooper just wasn't the type of man who expected other men to live up to his personal standards.

Which was good, Kunkle thought, because he had never met anyone who could have done so. *He* certainly couldn't.

Cooper drove them up an access ramp onto a thoroughfare as Kunkle continued to come down from his battle high. When he was breathing almost normally again, a thought struck him. He had just killed a number of men. Not as many as Cooper of course, but several just the same, and it had hardly been in the line of duty. The fact was he and Cooper had broken the law the minute they set foot on Dill's property. According to the law, they were both guilty of trespassing, burglary and even homicide.

Technically, they had broken the law. But with his emotions finally returning to normal, Kunkle was somewhat surprised to find that he felt no guilt. The laws of "man" might have been broken, but they had done nothing immoral. The New York Jets collection they had stolen had been obtained with money made in illegal ways, and the men they had shot had been thieves and murderers themselves.

A slight depression flowed over the detective. Matt Cooper was the man he, Greg Kunkle, knew he *should* have been.

Not as fast, or deadly, or smart maybe. But totally *moral*. He was the man Kunkle had tried to be when he first put on the NOPD uniform years ago. A man with a genuine passion for helping people and protecting the weak and innocent from the strong-but-evil. But gradually, step-by-step and little-by-little, he had lost his way. It had started when he first accepted free meals at restaurants. Then he found himself "fixing" traffic and parking tickets for the restaurants' owners.

No favor came without a price, Kunkle had realized even back then. And at that point, he should have quit and insisted on paying his way just like everyone else.

But he hadn't.

Soon after that, he'd started taking money to look the other way when drug deals went down. Then he'd purposely contaminated the chain of evidence on several criminal cases in return for money. On several occasions, he had even provided a safe police escort for illegal drugs and guns being driven from one spot to another. He had rationalized it all by telling himself that all cops did these things because they didn't get paid enough. And that rationalization had worked. At least for a while.

Cooper drove silently on. As Kunkle's thoughts continued to race, he realized that was one of the things he really liked about the man. He didn't speak unless he had something to say, and he'd bet his life that Cooper had never taken a bribe of any kind.

Kunkle's brain was spinning, and it returned suddenly to the revival, and the spiritual experience he'd had a little over a week earlier. He had, both literally and figuratively, stumbled upon the service. He had been drunk because the rationalizations for his actions were beginning to wear thin. But he had found himself accidentally driving past the large coliseum, noticing the thousands of people parking and walking toward the service. And for some reason he still couldn't quite define, he had pulled into the parking lot and joined them.

Kunkle remembered the music he had heard at the beginning of the service. Then a prayer that centered around the
destruction caused by Hurricane Katrina. The storm had hit
the city years earlier, but many New Orleans residents were
still reeling from the decimation it had brought. And it was to
them that the night's offering would go. When the plates were
passed, Kunkle had been surprised to find himself pulling the
last two twenty-dollar bills from his money clip and dropping
them into the plate with the other coins and bills.

Which had made no sense to him at all—not even as he did
it. It meant he would not be able to drop by the liquor store on
his way home after the service.

Then the preacher had taken the pulpit. He had spoken
calmly and sincerely—without any of the "fire and brim-
stone" Kunkle had half-expected. And it was during this
sermon that the alcohol he had consumed earlier had begun
to wear off. And, with it, had gone the last of the false rationalizations to which the detective was clinging so desperately.

Suddenly, Kunkle felt as if he was standing naked before
both God and men, his sins tattooed all over his body for the
entire world—and heaven—to see.

Tears had begun pouring from his eyes. And when the
sermon ended, and the invitation to accept Christ as his
personal savior was given, Kunkle had found himself walking down the aisle with hundreds of other sinners, eager to
seek redemption and the inner peace he could no longer find
through alcohol or other artificial means.

Ever since that night, Kunkle knew that his heart and soul
belonged to Jesus. But his brain had been an addled mass of
questions he seemed unable to work through.

"We're here."

Cooper's words cut abruptly into Kunkle's thoughts, and
the detective realized he had lapsed into another of the semi-
trances to which he seemed drawn since the revival. He looked

up to see the back door to the Hotel Lafitte through the windshield in front of him. Slowly, he turned toward Cooper.

"What do you want me to do?" he asked.

Bolan was frowning slightly, as if he sensed the intensity of Kunkle's thoughts. "Go inside, get some rest and wait for me," the big man said. "Drink as much water as you can. These sort of things dehydrate you. I'll either come by or call after I take this stuff to McFarley." He nodded toward the suitcases in the backseat.

"Okay," Kunkle said as he got out of the car. Then, just before he closed it behind him, he stuck his head back in. "Have you decided to trust me yet, Cooper?" he asked bluntly.

The man took a few seconds to answer, and during that time Kunkle could almost see the wheels turning behind his furrowed eyebrows. Finally, the big fighter behind the wheel of the Escalade spoke. "I think you should start calling me Matt," he finally said.

Kunkle was so flooded with emotion that he merely nodded, then closed the door. Fishing his room key out of the side pocket of his sport coat, he turned to watch for just a second as Cooper drove away.

And as he opened the back door to the hotel, he felt as if a huge burden had been lifted from his heart.

16

By the time the Bolan returned to his condo it was nearly
0500 in the morning. Shedding his blacksuit, weapons and
other gear, he set the two packed suitcases containing the Jets
paraphernalia next to the desk, then sat down on the side of
the bed.

Bolan couldn't help yawning as he lifted his wrist and set
the alarm buzzer on his chronograph for one hour. Then he
lay down on his side.

The next thing he was aware of was the alarm going off.
He twisted on the bed, cut the noise with the push of a button
and stood up.

By the time he had showered and shaved it was almost
0730. He glanced toward the suitcases from Bill Dill's house,
then opened one of his own bags, pulling out a blue shirt,
khaki pants and a brown corduroy sport coat. The Beretta
went beneath his arm again in the shoulder rig, and the Desert
Eagle took its usual place on his hip. But he didn't forget
the Cold Steel Espada or the little NAA Pug mini-revolver.
He clipped the big Spanish folding knife into his waistband
behind his back, and shoved the Pug down inside his underwear on his "weak hand" side.

The drive to Lake Pontchartrain took almost an hour in the

early-morning traffic. But by the time he got there, Bolan saw that the parking lot was already half full. Men and boys working the night shift at fish canneries and other New Orleans businesses were already heading into the brothel on the lower floors for an "eye opener."

Felix O'Banion met Bolan the second he stepped into the old mansion.

"Tommy up yet?" Bolan asked. He remembered McFarley making it clear he wasn't a morning person.

"He hasn't been to bed yet," O'Banion said in his thick Irish brogue. "He's been waiting for you." Then, without another word, the Irishman led the way down the hall.

The soldier lugged the two suitcases along behind the man, then stepped into the elevator. A moment later, they were on the top floor and the doors were rolling open. O'Banion stepped off of the elevator, pointed toward McFarley's door down the hall, then got back on. The doors closed again, and Bolan was left standing alone, half-surprised that he hadn't been searched for weapons again.

It was a good sign. It meant that he had finally gained McFarley's trust.

Bolan had to set one of the suitcases down in order to twist the knob on McFarley's door. Picking it back up by the handle, he shouldered the door the rest of the way open and crossed the empty outer office. He still had not met McFarley's secretary, and he hoped he wouldn't. The photographs, plants and other items covering her desk led him to believe that she was an older, at least somewhat innocent, woman.

Eventually, she would be out of a job because Bolan was going to kill Tommy McFarley. But he had no desire to see her go down in the process.

Bolan set the suitcases down again as he opened the door to McFarley's office. He found the New Orleans crime boss seated behind his desk. The man was in the process of opening the middle drawer of his desk, and Bolan remembered the Webley he'd seen earlier.

The soldier pulled the suitcases inside as McFarley produced what looked like a gold-plated fingernail clipper. Evidently, word of Cooper's success had already reached the Irishman; and Bolan wondered if the burglary and gunfight might even have made the news.

Without preamble, McFarley said, "You didn't find Namath's ring?"

"No," Bolan replied as he dropped the suitcases to the floor directly in front of McFarley's desk. He stared at the man as the criminal kingpin went to work on his fingernails. He was tempted to just draw the Desert Eagle and kill McFarley where he sat, but it was still too early. First, he needed to disrupt at least one of the man's connections so that his operations would be left in chaos when he died. Eventually, Bolan knew that the various factions of criminal activity might come together again under someone else, or restructure as smaller operations independent of a central governing leader. It would be impossible to stop that from happening—there was always more evil ready to step up to the plate to fill the void when a player was removed. But he could delay that day for a long time if he scrambled some of McFarley's infrastructure before he killed the man.

So Bolan just stared at the man. "My guess," he said, "is that Dill never had Namath's ring. That story has all of the earmarks of an urban legend. Joe's Super Bowl ring would be the ultimate prize for a Jets fan, and it seems logical that such an exaggeration would eventually creep into the tale. Dill himself might even have started it."

McFarley nodded as he continued to shorten his fingernails with the golden clipper. "Let's see what you *did* get," he said.

Bolan unzipped the two suitcases, then began distributing their contents throughout the office on chairs, side tables and McFarley's desk. He'd not had time to look at the items closely when he and Kunkle had loaded them, but took in the memorabilia as he pulled out both green and white jerseys, autographed and dated thigh and knee pads, chinstraps, miniature helmets and ticket stubs. Many of the souvenirs bore Joe Namath's autograph. Others had been signed by other Jets, both current and retired.

"Not a bad haul," McFarley said when Bolan had finished. "Not bad at all. Not that I want this crap myself." He curved the clipper around a thumb and a tiny speck of nail sailed up into the air. "I just didn't want Dill to have them." The chuckle he let out could only be described as obscene.

"Well, you've got them whether you want them or not," Bolan said as he placed an autographed football on McFarley's desk. Glancing down, he saw the big black X stamped next to the brand logo. The X meant the ball had actually been used in a game.

"You did even better than I'd expected," McFarley said. "You killed Dill and a houseful of his men. I doubt that there's anyone left in his organization with the skills to take over, which means they'll be running around like chickens with their heads cut off."

"Anxiously looking for a leader," Bolan finished for the man. He straightened in front of the desk. "And I wonder just who that new leader might be?" There was a trace of sarcasm in his voice.

"Correct you are, boyo," McFarley said. Smiling widely, he finally dropped the fingernail clipper back into his drawer and slid it closed. "They'll be more than happy to switch sides." He grunted out a short laugh. "Or maybe under these circumstances I should say *teams*. I'll just add Dill's operations to everything else I've got going."

Bolan placed his hands on his hips. "I didn't figure this little errand was simply another test of my loyalty," he said. "Oh, it was definitely that all right, but it was also to get rid of Dill."

McFarley's smile still covered his whole face. "I knew it was a distinct possibility," he said. "And it was a much appreciated dividend. I understand you shot him in bed."

Bolan paused for a moment. He doubted that detail had been leaked to the press. It was exactly the kind of information the police held back to help identify suspects during the investigation that would follow. Knowledge of such things helped separate the true suspects from the inevitable "crazies" who always came forward and claimed responsibility for high profile cases.

Which meant McFarley had his own plant within Dill's operation. Probably the same man who had drawn the crude blueprints of the house. There was simply no other explanation for his knowing such details.

"So," Bolan finally said. "I've got to ask you. Are we through playing these silly little grade-school games yet? Or do you have more hoops you want me to jump through before you trust me?"

McFarley sat back in his chair and clasped his hands behind his neck. "You noticed you got in here without being frisked, didn't you?" he said.

"I noticed," Bolan said.

Well," McFarley said, "that should answer your question. Not to mention the fact that you committed a first-degree burglary, and I don't know how many homicides for me." He took in a long breath, then let it out slowly. "Cops, Feds, whatever, would never be allowed to do that. The law's run at me every way in the book so far. But no department or agency would sign off on a spectacle like you put on last night in order to get an undercover man in with *anyone*."

Bolan let a thin smile creep across his face. "No, they wouldn't," he said honestly. "So now you've also got a hammer to hold over my head. There must be a thousand ways you could get word to the cops that it was me who shot up Dill's place last night. Ways you could let them know without involving yourself, of course."

"Of course." McFarley grinned back at him. "But it wasn't *just* you at Dill's last night."

Bolan knew immediately that word of Kunkle's involvement had also reached the Big Easy crime boss. Had the plant recognized Kunkle through his disguise? Or did he simply know that Bolan had recruited a partner for the strike? Before he said any more about it, Bolan needed to let McFarley reveal more about just how much he knew.

"What's that supposed to mean?" he asked.

"I didn't mention it earlier," McFarley said, "because, like you said, this was still another test for you. But I've had my own informant inside Dill's operation for some time now."

"I'd guessed that," Bolan said. "You already know too many details of what went on inside the house that wouldn't have made the news."

"Right you are," McFarley said. "I tipped off my man that you were coming, and he hid in the basement during the whole thing." The crime boss crossed his arms behind his head and wheeled his chair in closer to his desk. "My man *did* catch a few glimpses of the action, however. You had some guy with you who was bald on top but had a short blond ponytail and goatee." He leaned in over his desk and the grin on his face disappeared. "My man said there was something familiar about him, but he couldn't place him." Dropping his arms from behind his head, McFarley clasped his hands together in front of him, then continued. "Who was this guy?"

Bolan met the man's stare with one of his own. "An old Army buddy of mine," he said. "He's helped me out before, and I wanted someone watching my back last night."

"How come he looked familiar to my guy?" McFarley demanded.

Bolan answered the question with one of his own. "How should I know? My man doesn't work for you, but he works the same side of the law you do. It seems likely that their paths might cross now and again."

McFarley nodded. "Okay. *You* hired him, *you* pay him," he said. Leaning down, he pulled out one of the bottom drawers of his desk.

As he waited, Bolan remembered passing the stairs to the basement as he and Kunkle left Dill's house a few hours earlier. And he remembered the hand-drawn map of Dill's house. The basement was conspicuously absent from the drawing.

Exactly how an informant would have presented it if he planned to hide out there to avoid being killed.

As he waited on McFarley, Bolan wondered just what the man was about to produce from the drawer. It might be money for a job done even better than he'd expected. On the other hand, if the Irishman's snitch in the basement had actually seen through Kunkle's new look and named him, the crime boss might well be preparing to pull out the British Webley revolver and add the Executioner's brain matter to the traces of whoever's had been on the office wall the first time Bolan had been there.

The soldier slowly inched a hand up his lapel, ready to throw back the tail of his jacket and draw the Desert Eagle.

But a few moments later, a stack of green hundred-dollar bills, secured in a brown paper wrapper, sat on McFarley's desktop. "I'd planned on giving you ten grand for your time if you came through," the kingpin said as he shoved the money across the desk toward Bolan. "Here it is. Cut it up with your man any way you want. But that's all you get."

"Fair enough," Bolan said as he lifted the stack of bills, then dropped them into the left side pocket of his corduroy sport coat.

McFarley leaned to his side and pressed an intercom button on his phone. Apparently the kingpin's secretary had arrived for the workday. He heard an older woman, with a somewhat hoarse voice, say, "Yes, Tommy?"

"Send Felix in here," McFarley said.

Seconds later, the door opened and O'Banion—the last of McFarley's personal aides and bodyguards—entered the room. He stood as if at attention during some military ceremony as he waited on his boss's next orders.

"Take Cooper into your office, Felix," McFarley said. "Fill him in on our situation at the boxing matches tonight. Then send him back in here before he leaves."

O'Banion frowned, his gray and white eyebrows lowering over his eyes. "Excuse me, Tommy," he said in his thick brogue, "but I thought it was going to be *me* you sent to—"

"Well, you thought wrong then, Felix," McFarley said abruptly. "Now, do as you're told."

For a moment, O'Banion stood where he was. Then, with a look of resignation on his face, he turned and walked out of the office.

The soldier followed.

17

The club was so filled with cigar and cigarette smoke that Bolan wondered how the boxers could even breathe.

Next to him, in the back row of seats, Felix O'Banion added his own cigar smoke to the pollution. Far in the distance, Bolan watched as two featherweights danced around each other, tentatively throwing left jabs that were occasionally followed by a right cross, hook or uppercut. It was round three but, so far, neither man had been willing to completely open up and go for broke.

And the crowd didn't like it.

Boos and hisses came from the men and women sitting in the rows in front of Bolan and O'Banion. Mixed in with the sounds were occasional words like "Box!" and "Fight, dammit!" But they seemed to have no effect on the men in the ring.

Bolan wasn't bothered by the poor showing on the canvas. The fact was, he didn't care about this fight at all.

It was the next bout that concerned him.

The main card of the evening called for another heavyweight match between two old club fighters who had mixed it up several times in years gone by. Wimpy Booth had won four of his previous fights with Trevor Clark and was the favored man at odds of three-to-one. But McFarley was counting on Booth to take a dive, so he had bet heavily on Clark.

Word of what had happened the week before to the boxer and his manager who had ignored McFarley's orders was widespread within the club-fighting world. And no one in the know expected Booth to do anything but hit the canvas.

Even if he had to knock himself out to get it done.

Bolan leaned into O'Banion and raised his voice over the noise of the crowd. "How'd he get the name Wimpy?" he asked.

O'Banion chuckled, but it was forced. He didn't like Cooper or the quick rise the man had ridden toward the top of McFarley's operations. "Got it as a teenager," the Irishman said. "He used to get so nervous that he puked before every match. The other fighters started calling him Wimpy back then."

Bolan nodded, then turned his eyes back to the ring. That had to have been some time ago, he realized as he continued to watch the boring fight in front of him. He'd caught a glimpse of Wimpy Booth when they'd entered the club earlier, and the man had to be pushing forty. His days in the ring were numbered, so Bolan suspected he would be more than willing to take the dive and the large payoff McFarley would have offered for it.

But McFarley had not forgotten the double cross of the previous week, either. And Bolan and O'Banion were at the fight just in case Wimpy won. The crime boss wanted to send an immediate message this time.

If Booth won, Bolan was to shoot him before the referee even raised his hand in victory, which was why Bolan and O'Banion were in the back row. The club was not that big, and Bolan could easily draw the sound-suppressed Beretta and send a semiauto round into the man's shaved head, then disappear out the back with the Irishman before the rest of the crowd even realized what had happened.

As the fighters continued to dance and the crowd kept on

booing, Bolan's mind traveled back to his earlier meeting with McFarley. It had occurred right after O'Banion had explained to him what they'd be doing this night, and McFarley's fellow countryman had not been present.

McFarley had given Bolan a second assignment for the evening. It was an assignment that Bolan was to carry out regardless of what Wimpy Booth did in the ring. A duty he had not anticipated, and one that had all but shocked him. But the more he'd thought about it, the more it made sense. At least from McFarley's point of view.

McFarley believed he had discovered a true gem in his new man, Cooper. And he intended to restructure his entire criminal empire around that valuable commodity.

"You pull off these last two things for me," McFarley had assured Bolan, "and then I'm promoting you to the big time. Which means maybe a million bucks an assignment instead of the pennies you've been getting."

Bolan had forced a smile, feigning just the right amount of excitement—no more, no less—for a man who was confident in his own abilities.

The third round of the five-round match ended, and the fighters walked to their corners amid the jeers of the audience. The seconds wiped the sweat off their faces with towels and held water bottles to their lips. Water boys held up funnel-topped cans so the featherweights could wash their mouths out, then spit into them. A minute later, the bell sounded and they were on their feet again.

The dancing and fancy footwork continued, but few punches were thrown. The crowd grew even more angry and loud. Bolan studied the faces of the two men. The one named Jordan, wearing black trunks, was starting to grimace as the insults kept flying from down below. The other man, named Davis and wearing white, looked more oblivious to the crowd.

Bolan could have predicted what was about to happen even though no fix was in on this fight.

As the man in black's face grew tighter, the white-trunked fighter suddenly lunged forward, throwing a flurry of hooks at his opponent. The man in black covered his face with his gloves, using his elbows to protect his ribs and midsection. Letting the blows glance harmlessly off his arms, he backed up slowly until he was against the ropes, then pulled himself in even tighter as the onslaught of punches continued.

Gradually, the arms of the man wearing the white trunks began to slow. Then they dropped slightly, until his blows were all landing near the other fighter's elbows. Finally, they dropped to his side for a much needed rest.

Jordan didn't hesitate. As soon as he saw the other man's gloves go down he stepped in with a left jab, then a right cross. Both punches struck Davis full in the face, snapping his head backward each time. Then, as Davis raised his gloves to protect his head, Jordan went to work on his opponent's midsection, striking the man repeatedly in the upper chest—right over the heart. Gradually, Davis's gloves began to drop again as the blows disrupted the rhythm of the rapidly beating, blood-pumping organ.

The crowd was cheering finally, happy that something—*anything*—was finally happening. As Jordan's punches continued to jar Davis's chest, they screamed for blood.

And Jordan didn't disappoint them.

With Davis finally back-pedaling away from him, Jordan followed, still striking up under his opponent's raised gloves with uppercuts to the chest. When Davis finally stopped with his back against the ropes, Jordan took a half step back, then sent a right hook solidly into the man's jaw.

A split second later Davis was on the canvas and the referee was counting him out.

The crowd went wild.

In the midst of the celebration, a girl in a bikini, carrying a tray of plastic cups filled with beer, entered the club area. O'Banion stopped her, took two of the cups off the tray, then smiled as he folded a ten-dollar bill and stuck it in her cleavage.

The girl smiled back with a well-practiced, forced grin.

Bolan took one of the cups from O'Banion and pressed it to his lips. One watered-down beer wasn't going to interfere with what he had to do this night, and it would look strange to his companion if he turned it down.

The next fight came and went with more action but no knockout. As he pretended to watch the fighters, Bolan went over the best way to handle the two duties he needed to perform. If Wimpy went along with the plan, the first action wouldn't even have to be taken. But if he didn't, Bolan would have to shoot him with the sound-suppressed Beretta. And he had been ordered to do it while the man was still in the ring—in front of an audience—in order to further publicize McFarley's deadly reach and ruthlessness. Then, he'd have to get out of there before the police and security guards working the fights could pinpoint where the shot had come from.

Not easy.

No, Bolan thought, as he watched the two exit the ring, their fight over. The beer was no problem at all. The real problem he faced was what he was going to do if Booth decided to win his fight with Trevor Clark. He certainly wasn't going to murder a man because he refused to throw a fight.

As Bolan drained the last of his beer and dropped the plastic cup on the floor at his feet, the crowd began to cheer once more. He looked up to see Booth come walking out of the dressing room and down the aisle to his side. The fighter was surrounded by his manager, a cut man, water boy and other members of his entourage. He wore green boxing trunks and had a towel over his shoulders. A hole had been cut out of the center, and the ragged garment was worn much like a serape. There was nothing fancy about Booth or his people. They simply walked down the aisle to the ring as if strolling in the park.

The announcer called out Booth's name and record over the loudspeaker. He had barely gotten the words out of his mouth when Trevor Clark and his attendants appeared at the back of another aisle. Unlike Booth, Clark was clad in a robe that might have come from the Broadway play *Joseph and the Amazing Technicolor Dreamcoat*. The men following Clark stood back, giving him room to prance and shadowbox his way down the aisle with the different, iridescent colors catching the smoky lighting like a moving rainbow. When he reached the ring, Clark reached up and grabbed the bottom rope as one of his men grasped the robe at the collar from behind. As he pulled himself up, the flashing robe came off and the fighter's black skin, slick with sweat, replaced the gaudy robe under the lights.

Clark began to shadowbox around the ring, mugging for the audience, amid a mixture of cheers and boos.

Bolan sat in his seat, going over what he needed to do in his head once more. If Booth hadn't gone down by the end of the third round, he was supposed to shoot him. But that, he wouldn't do. So he racked his brain, trying to come up with an alternate plan, or at least an excuse, for letting the innocent man live. And while he did, he continued to work out his plan for carrying out the second assignment McFarley had given him.

Bolan needn't have worried. Booth had heard of what had happened to the fighter who refused to take a dive the week before, and he was taking no chances. He shuffled flat-footed around the canvas as Clark threw punch after punch. Booth returned one halfheartedly here and there. But all-in-all, he looked like a man who'd been drugged before the fight.

And he had been. The drug was *fear*.

Ten seconds before the first round was to end, Clark threw a right cross that glanced off Booth's chin. It should have done little more than wake the man up out of his sluggish performance, but Booth threw himself to the canvas on his back and lay still.

Nearly all of the noise from the crowd had turned to boos. The dive was so obvious that even the least-initiated boxing fan could see it for what it was.

That wasn't going to make McFarley happy, Bolan knew. He would have expected a better performance.

But it did get Bolan off the hook about killing Booth.

The crowd was on its feet, jeering and hissing and screaming obscenities as the referee counted Booth out. Bolan glanced around him quickly. His first assignment of the night had taken care of itself.

It was time to carry out the second order McFarley had given him. And he would have no better chance of doing it unnoticed than this moment, while everyone at the fight was focused on the fraud going on in the ring.

Bolan reached behind him and grasped the end of the Cold Steel Espada in his waistband, behind the extra Desert Eagle magazine carrier. Pulling it straight up, he twisted it slightly to let the opening hook catch on the top of his belt. The seven and one-half inch blade snapped into place as Bolan turned toward O'Banion and caught the man reaching for his gun inside his sport coat, apparently with his own plan for Cooper on this night.

With one fast, smooth thrust, Bolan slid the Spanish blade through O'Banion's shirt, skin and into his chest. He felt a slight bump in his hand as the tip of the blade caught a rib, then skidded up and over it before penetrating the Irishman's heart.

O'Banion turned to look him in the eye, an expression of total shock and confusion on his face.

Bolan met the man's gaze as he pumped the blade up, then down, then quickly withdrew it, closing the tail of the jacket over the jet spray of blood that pumped from the wound. Bolan pressed the jacket tight, causing the blood flow to drip down to the tail and then onto the floor. As the heart bled out, he did a quick 360-degree visual of the crowd. The attention of the people in attendance at the fight was still fixed on the ring as they screamed and jeered. So, without further ado, Bolan sat O'Banion back down in his seat to die as he closed the blade of the knife and shuffled past the seated man to the aisle.

The crowd was still booing Wimpy Booth as the Executioner exited the club.

And if anyone had noticed what he'd done during the pandemonium, they weren't saying or doing anything about it.

"BILL GROGAN'S GOAT, BOYO!" McFarley nearly shouted as soon as Bolan had entered his office. "It sounds like things went off even better than I'd expected them to!"

Bolan stopped in front of McFarley's desk as the crime boss opened the middle drawer of his desk. The big Webley revolver with the pearl grips crossed Bolan's mind again, and his right hand automatically inched to his belt, where he could sweep back his jacket and draw the Desert Eagle.

But there was no need to do so.

McFarley's good humor was genuine rather than a ruse. When his hand reappeared from the drawer, it held only the gold nail clippers Bolan had seen earlier.

"So you've already heard what happened?" Bolan asked.

"Booth went down in the first round," McFarley said, nodding. "I understand he made quite a spectacle of himself. I suppose I should sign him up for some acting lessons. Sounds like the crowd didn't buy it."

"It wasn't the most convincing performance I've ever seen," Bolan said. "But no one will ever prove he took a dive. How much did you win?"

"Oh, not all *that* much," McFarley said. "Spread around among a half-dozen bookies, I'd say just under a million."

"Not bad for a night's work," Bolan said.

"Well, not much compared to my other endeavors," Mc-Farley said. "But I like to keep my hand in the boxing game. Reminds me of where I come from, know what I mean?"

The soldier nodded.

"By the way," McFarley went on, "you didn't do bad for your night's work, either. The real news is that your second objective was successful. No more Felix."

Bolan frowned. "I just walked in the door and haven't said a word about anything that happened at the fight. Where did you hear about O'Banion? Where are you getting all this information?"

McFarley laughed as he snipped at the nail on his thumb. "I had another man there, watching you. His job was to call in as soon as the fight was over and give me the details."

"So you're still watching me?" Bolan said, shaking his head in false disgust. In actuality, he was pleased with the way things had gone so far on this mission. Every test Mc-Farley had put him through had taken a few more miscreants off the streets and thrown a monkey wrench into one or more of McFarley's criminal pipelines. He just needed to disrupt the man's drug and gun smuggling ops and he could execute McFarley himself and be done with it.

But Bolan knew he still needed to play the part. So he said, "How many more hoops do I have to jump through before you finally trust me?"

"Oh, I do trust you," McFarley replied as he rolled his chair slightly back from the desk and brushed fingernail clippings from the top of his thighs. "It's just a policy I have. Any time I can have another of my men keeping an eye on someone I send out on a job, I do it." He paused as he switched the clippers from his thumb to his index finger. "You'll do the same—watch my other men on occasion—sooner or later." Finishing with the nail clipper, he dropped it back into the drawer and took out a pencil and a pen. Slowly and quietly, he began tapping them on the desktop as if he were playing the drums to some unheard melody. "But tell me. Why the knife on Felix? That meant a lot of blood. Why not just shoot him with that silencer gun of yours?"

"You've obviously never shot someone at point-blank range before," Bolan said.

"Well," McFarley said. "No I haven't. At least not personally."

"Shooting a man up close blows out more blood than a quick thrust and pump with a knife," Bolan replied. "Especially since I could use my other hand to cover the wound with his coat."

McFarley squinted at the Executioner. "You've still got a little blood on your hands. And a bit on your shirt."

"Not nearly as much as if I'd shot him," Bolan said simply.

"I like it," McFarley said as he continued to beat his rhythm with the pen and pencil. "I like it. And the way you did it'll get around. Stabbed him right there in the midst of who-knows-how-many people. Sort of a variation of the old 'hiding in plain sight' principle."

"It worked out well," Bolan said. "Everybody will know who was behind it but again, they won't be able to prove it. Now, tell me just one thing. You and O'Banion go way back if I'm not mistaken. I might almost say you were friends. So why'd you want him dead?"

For a second, McFarley almost looked sad. "Enforcers for a business like mine are a lot like boxers," he finally said. "They get old. They aren't as good at their jobs as they once had been. It becomes necessary to get rid of them."

"Well," Bolan said, "do me a favor. When I get too old, just let me know and I'll fade away into the sunset on my own. Won't even ask for a pension."

The words brought laughter to the Irishman's face again. "We've got a long time before that becomes an issue," he said.

"Then fill me in on the current issues," Bolan said. "You

mentioned something about big money coming my way instead of the peanuts I've been working for."

"Right you are, boyo," McFarley said. "Why don't you take a chair and we'll talk?"

Bolan took two steps to his right and dropped down into a stuffed armchair. "What have you got?" he asked.

"A problem that originated in Colombia," McFarley said. "I had three million dollars' worth of cocaine flying into the swamps. Coast Guard planes picked them up and they had to drop the whole bundle over the Gulf of Mexico."

"And...?" Bolan prompted.

"*And* I hold the position that the Colombians owe me the three million bucks," McFarley said, still working on his fingernails. "It was their fault they got caught."

"Let me guess the rest," Bolan said. "They say the loss was unavoidable, and blame you for not paying off the right people or otherwise ensuring that the shipment got through."

"Right on the nose," McFarley said. "So what I want you to do is go to Colombia—"

"—and get your three million dollars back," Bolan finished for him.

"Not exactly," McFarley said, finally putting down the pen and pencil and ending his drum roll. "I want *four* million. The fourth is for interest and what the civil courts call mental anguish."

"Not to mention the fact that it'll show that you don't screw with Tommy McFarley," Bolan added.

"Precisely," the criminal kingpin said. "It shouldn't be hard. I've played nicey-nice with Eduardo Guzman—he's the cartel leader I deal with. I've phoned and told him not to worry, that I'm sending one of my best men down there to negotiate a settlement. I happen to know he keeps around thirty million dollars, U.S., in a safe in his office. Just take four. I don't want to close down that pipeline. In spite of this recent disagreement, he's been a good man to work with. So don't take more than the four million. But leave the rest of the money stacked on his desk so that whoever finds it will get the message. I've laid the groundwork. You should be able to get in with no trouble."

"How about getting out again?" Bolan asked.

"That could get a little trickier," McFarley said. "Since you're going to kill him to add the icing on the cake of my message."

Bolan stared at the man. "I've heard of Guzman," he said honestly—Stony Man Farm had an entire file on the cartel man. "He'll have guards around me all of the time."

"So you'll kill them, too." McFarley shrugged. "You've proved you can take care of yourself when you're outnumbered."

"They're going to pat me down just like your own men did when I first started coming here."

"So you slip a weapon past them. You've proved you can do that already, too. Or you can find a weapon inside his office—I'm sure he'll have something. You can always just kill him with your bare hands if you're alone in the office with him. I've got a feeling you know how to do that as well."

"I do," Bolan said. "But I don't want to try to kill all of his men empty-handed."

McFarley waved a hand across his face as if the statement was nothing. "You can pick up guns on your way out," he said.

Bolan frowned. "Like I said, I've heard of Guzman. I'll have to get back to the airport and completely out of the country before I'm beyond his reach."

"That you will, boyo, that you will." McFarley leaned into his desk and smiled. "But the risk is worth the payoff. That fourth million? It's for you when you get back."

"I can't fly commercial, you know."

"I know," McFarley said. "I've got a private plane and a pilot ready to take off as soon as you are."

Bolan shook his head. "No way," he said. "I don't know your man or your plane. I have a guy I've used in the past who I know I can trust. It's my head on the chopping block here, Tommy. I either use him or I don't go."

A look of doubt clouded the crime boss's face for a moment, then he finally nodded. "Okay. You feel more comfortable with your own man, you use him. But whatever cut he gets, and the expenses, come out of *your* million."

"It's worth the cost," Bolan said. "So let me make sure I've got everything straight. I fly to Colombia, lose my weapons to Guzman's guards, go into his office and get him to open the safe. I take four million bucks and stack the rest on the desk, and somewhere in there I kill him. Either with a weapon I've snuck past his men or in some other way. Then I get out of his house however I can, get to the airport, fly back to you with the money, and keep a million for myself—minus my pilot's fee and plane expenses." He paused. "Have I got it all right?"

"You've got it all right," McFarley repeated. "Any more questions?"

"Yeah," the Executioner said. "You don't happen to have a red cape with a great big *S* on it I can wear trying to pull all this off, do you?"

McFarley burst into laughter. "I know it's risky," he said. "But a million dollars is a million dollars. And you've proved that if anyone can do all this, it's you. Sorry there's no cape. But look on the bright side."

"I'm not sure there is a bright side in all this."

"Sure there is," McFarley said. "You may not have Superman's cape but if Guzman happens to have any Kryptonite on hand, you aren't allergic to it."

The Executioner nodded slowly. "No," he said. "I'm not allergic to Kryptonite. Just lead."

18

"You know, Sarge," Jack Grimaldi said from behind the controls of one of the Learjet. "You never cease to surprise me."

Bolan, dressed in a lightweight white suit and a burgundy shirt, open at the collar, turned to his long-time friend. "How's that?" he asked.

"McFarley has his own planes and pilots. I'm just surprised he didn't make you use one of them."

Bolan chuckled. "This whole op has pretty much been Mc-Farley and me feeling each other out," he said. "The man's not stupid—he's tested me over and over. Granted, those tests have allowed me to put down a bunch of bad guys, but they've been tests of loyalty, nonetheless."

"And this is another test?" Grimaldi asked.

"Of sorts," Bolan said. "It's a real assignment, of course. Actually all of the tests have included real assignments that profited the man. He wanted to see just how far outside the law I'd go. Now, he not only wants his money back, he wants to see if I'm willing to work outside the bounds of the U.S. in a country where no U.S. federal agent has any jurisdiction."

Grimaldi grasped the microphone from the control panel in front of him. They had passed over Panama a few minutes earlier, and the pilot advised the tower that he would be requesting to land in Bogotá.

The Executioner looked out through the windshield for a moment and saw the towering Andes Mountains in the distance. Then he leaned back in his seat and closed his eyes for a few moments. He had been in Colombia more times than he could remember.

In the eighties and nineties, the Medellín Cartel, headed by Pablo Escobar, had exercised a near stranglehold on cocaine coming into the United States. But, as inevitably happened to such large drug operations, other syndicates had wanted a piece of the action and gradually chipped away at it. And while it hadn't put an end to Escobar's business, he had been forced to decrease it somewhat after he was finally arrested.

Bolan couldn't help but shake his head in awe at the dishonesty and stupidity of the way the Colombian courts had handled Escobar. He had been assigned to country-club type prison of his own design and allowed to do pretty much as he pleased. For a time. He escaped and was eventually shot and killed in a gun battle.

Another thing that had slowed the Colombian traffic was that their government had been pressured hard by the U.S. to take action on the coca leaf growers. In the past, the only times they hadn't "looked the other way" was when they were accepting their payoffs. A lot of that had been halted since, and special Colombian narcoterrorist tactical teams and undercover operatives, working hand-in-hand with the American Drug Enforcement Administration, went on frequent search-and-destroy missions to eradicate the crops and arrest the guilty.

But even with all of these efforts, cocaine continued to flow steadily out of Colombia into the U.S. And while the Colombian trade had faded slightly, countries like Peru and Bolivia had been ready and waiting to fill in the gaps. Often, regardless of where it was grown, the coke came through

Mexico these days, and the competition between the Mexican cartels had produced unprecedented violence all over America's southern neighbor. Especially at the border areas. And it was finally spilling over into California, Arizona, New Mexico and other states.

Had Bolan been the kind of man who allowed himself to get depressed, these thoughts would have been enough to do it. It seemed that partially solving the Colombian problem had done little but shift the drug traffic to other points of origin.

But Bolan was no quitter. Giving up simply wasn't in his DNA. And he would not cease his pursuit of *anyone* smuggling illegal drugs until every tiny nook and cranny of the business had been destroyed.

Or they destroyed him.

Looking out through the windshield of the Learjet again, Bolan saw glimpses of Bogotá. The city was sheltered by a ring of mountains, some of which grew a precipitous two thousand feet in the air. Grimaldi was on the radio again as he flew over the jagged rock, then began a quick descent toward a private runway on the east side of the huge airport.

Bolan closed his eyes once more. He had left Kunkle back at the Hotel Lafitte with a week's worth of groceries and money to pay the manager. The born-again New Orleans cop had wanted to come along, but Bolan was afraid someone they met in Bogotá might recognize him. McFarley had made it clear that almost everyone he did business with had spent time with the prostitutes on the lower floors of his old plantation house, and Bolan saw no reason to take any chances.

Bolan's eyelids lifted again when the tires hit the runway. Grimaldi slowed the plane to a crawl, then stopped it all together when the order to do so came over the radio.

The soldier looked out to see a Colombian army jeep heading toward them. The man driving wore the uniform of a colonel. The other two men were dressed in civvies. One wore a white suit similar to Bolan's, while the other was dressed in light blue-and-white-striped seersucker.

"Looks like your taxi's here," Grimaldi said. "Sure you don't want me to come with you?"

"Uh-uh, Jack," Bolan said as his hand reached for the door handle. "McFarley told them there would be one man coming alone. I don't want to do anything out of the ordinary that might arouse their curiosity. At least not until I have to."

"Okay," Grimaldi said. "But killing Guzman is going to be a little off the flight plan."

"Yeah," Bolan said. "From there on, it'll be a race to see if I can get back here and we can lift off before we become lead magnets."

Grimaldi smiled and shook his head. "If it was anybody but you, big guy," he said, "I'd bow out of this assignment right now."

"No you wouldn't," Bolan replied as he swung open the door. "You'd do the same for Able Team or Phoenix Force, or any other warriors you were fighting with. You're as much a soldier as any of us, Jack. And you'd do what was right."

"Okay," Grimaldi said. "But you do the shooting on this one. I'll do the flying."

"You've got a deal." Bolan disembarked from the plane and turned to pull a small suitcase after him. By the time he had turned, the jeep had stopped at his side.

The colonel stayed behind the wheel. The two men in lightweight suits got out.

"We speak very good English," were the first words out of the mouth of the man in the white suit. He was tall for a South American, and had bleached blond hair that was as fake-looking as Kunkle's ponytail and contrasted sharply with his olive-colored skin.

"And I speak decent Spanish," Bolan said. "So we ought to be able to understand each other one way or another."

The man in the seersucker suit stepped forward. He was

shorter but with wider shoulders, and had stubby dark curls for hair. "I am afraid we must disarm you before we go any further," he said.

Bolan had expected that. So he dropped his bag, raised his arms and waited while the cartel man patted him down and removed the Desert Eagle, the Beretta, and finally the knife. Bolan glanced at the colonel still in the jeep. The man had turned his face away, staring off into the distance in order to avoid seeing the weapons violation.

It might have slowed down some, Bolan thought again as he waited, but payoffs were still happening in Colombia.

"And now, *señor*," seersucker-wearing man said, "the little baby gun you are known to hide on your body."

As quickly as a flash of lightning, Bolan knew that McFarley had to have provided the Guzman mob with the information on the North American Arms .22 Magnum revolver. There was no other way they could have known about it. But what did that mean?

Had his cover been burned somehow? Had McFarley set him up to be killed?

Or had McFarley given that information in order to further the guise that he was there to work out a peaceful solution? If so, why hadn't he let Bolan in on that aspect of the plan?

The Executioner wasn't sure, but the only thing he could do at this point was play along with the game.

Letting a smile cross his face, Bolan reached just behind his belt buckle where he'd secreted the NAA Pug and pulled it out. "You guys are thorough," he said as he handed it to the shorter of the two men. "I'll give you that."

"Gracias," the man in the seersucker suit said. "And now…" He stepped back, bowed slightly at the waist and waved his arm dramatically for Bolan to get into the jeep.

He complied, taking a seat behind the colonel.

A moment later, the two cartel men pulled themselves up and into the jeep. The colonel took off across the runways and access roads of the airport, finally stopping behind a new Mercedes-Benz in a parking lot next to the terminal. It reminded Bolan of the car he and Kunkle had taken from Bill Dill's house to return to the Cadillac.

Bolan watched as the tall blond man took a quick look around, then reached inside his jacket and pulled out an overstuffed white envelope. A flash of Colombian bills caught Bolan's eye beneath the flap as the colonel grabbed the envelope and hid it inside his uniform blouse.

No, Bolan thought again. Business might have slowed, but baksheesh certainly hadn't died out completely in Colombia.

The two cartel men and Bolan transferred to the Mercedes, with the Executioner in the backseat. They remained silent as the blond man guided the vehicle off the airport grounds.

Bolan was slightly surprised when the driver navigated them away from the city, to the north. If he remembered correctly, that area consisted of salt mines left from an earlier age when a mountain lake had once covered Bogotá.

Bolan leaned forward. "Where are we going?" he asked.

The man behind the wheel of the Mercedes spoke out of the side of his mouth. "You'll see," he said. "Just a friendly meeting place where you can speak with Don Eduardo."

Bolan leaned back in his seat. There was nothing he could do at this point. But he had kept track of his weapons since they'd been taken from him, and had made note of the man wearing seersucker shoving the Desert Eagle into his belt and handing the blond man the Beretta. The .22 Magnum Pug had gone into the one man's right front pocket, and the Beretta—still complete with sound suppressor—was lying on the front seat between the two men. The tall blond man had dropped the Espada knife into his right front pocket.

The Mercedes slowed as it passed through a small mountain village, and Bolan saw a sign that identified it as Zipaquirá. They passed more signs directing them to the underground Salt Cathedral, formed where salt had been mined by members of the Chibcha tribe.

Everyone they passed in the village took a look at the Mercedes-Benz, then looked quickly away. It was obvious that the car was known—and feared—and that the residents wanted nothing to do with it.

Roughly a mile from the village, the blond cartel man turned the wheel and drove the car into another dark mine tunnel. The smell of salt grew strong in Bolan's nostrils as the Mercedes twisted and turned for perhaps another quarter mile. The only light came from the headlights, but it was enough to finally spot another, almost identical, Mercedes facing them.

The blond man slowed the automobile, then stopped. "Let's go," he said over his shoulder as he and the other man vacated the front.

Bolan opened the door and got out of the backseat. He had expected a meeting in an office or home—not a salt mine, and he had expected to still have the NAA Pug on him at this point, too. But both of those expectations had proved faulty, which meant he would have to improvise.

The two men who had picked him up at the airport each took one of his arms and guided him toward the Mercedes. Four more men had gotten out of that car, and each cradled either an M-16 assault rifle or a Heckler & Koch MP-5 submachine gun. A stubby, shadowy form could still be seen in the backseat.

One of the men with the H&Ks opened the back door and directed Bolan to get in. But before he could comply, the dark shadow in the back said, "You have checked him well for weapons?"

"We have, Don Eduardo," the man in the seersucker suit replied.

The man in the back waved Bolan in and motioned for him to shut the door behind him. When he had, Bolan found that he and Eduardo Guzman were in semidarkness, illuminated only by the headlights of the other Mercedes.

Guzman was eating pistachio nuts, cracking the shells in his teeth, then spitting the two halves onto the floor of the backseat as he chomped on the nut itself. Even in the darkness, Bolan could tell that the man was vastly overweight, and smelled of salt, pistachios and sweat.

The cartel leader offered the sack containing the nuts to the soldier, who shook his head. "No, thanks," he said.

"Then we should get right down to business," Guzman said. "Your McFarley blames me for not being more careful in my delivery. I blame him for not properly bribing the correct U.S. Coast Guard officials to ensure that my product came through." He grunted, then shoved another pistachio into his mouth.

Bolan heard a crunch, then a sickeningly wet sound as the two halves of the shell flew from Guzman's mouth, hit the back of the front seat, then fell to the floor. In the dim light, the soldier could see spots on Guzman's pants. Squinting, he saw that they were pistachio shells that had failed to fall all the way to the floor and stuck to the cartel man's slacks.

The Executioner pried his eyes away from the sweating man and glanced through the windows of the Mercedes. The six men with Guzman had taken up positions around the car. There was absolutely no way Bolan could kill the cartel leader and get away. Besides which, he knew that Guzman would not have brought the money from his safe along with him in this elaborate setup.

"So," Guzman said around another mouthful of nuts, "who is to say who is at fault?"

Bolan decided to play along as the rest of his mind tried to figure out a plan of action. "Well, Don Eduardo," he said quietly, "it's a little different in America. Paying off cops and military personnel there is tricky. It's much more difficult trying to decide who's susceptible to a bribe and who's not.

And if you try to pay off the wrong guy, you're headed for prison." His eyes skirted the outside of the vehicle again. All of the men leaned against the car, their backs against the windows to allow their leader the privacy he had to have ordered. But they still cradled their weapons in their arms.

The Executioner knew he was fast, and he knew he was skilled in unarmed combat. But being unarmed in this situation, he didn't know how he was going to take out six heavily armed men before one of them got to him.

"Bullshit," Guzman said. "Perhaps it is more difficult—American cops and servicemen are paid better and don't need to accept bribes. But here, it is expected. So who is to say which is wrong?"

He shoved the paper bag full of nuts toward Bolan again, and when he did, the soldier caught a glimpse of silver as his sport coat opened slightly. The item had been sticking out from under the man's left armpit and had caught a flash of light inside the Mercedes.

Was it a gun? Bolan couldn't be sure, but if it was, he saw a whole new strategy begin to form in his mind.

"I will return one-and-one-half million dollars to Senor McFarley," Guzman said as he continued cracking and chomping on his pistachios. "That is my one and only offer. We split the loss."

Bolan didn't speak for a moment. Then, finally, he said, "I'll have to talk to him first. Do you have the money with you?"

"I have one-and-a-half million," Guzman spit out along with a nutshell. "In the trunk. That is my one and final offer."

Bolan fell silent for a moment. Then, with a tone of exasperation, he said, "Well, the least you can do is offer me some more pistachios."

Guzman laughed in triumph. Then, as he extended the sack toward the big American, his jacket fell open again.

Bolan's hand shot under the jacket and into the man's

sweaty armpit. But it came out holding a nickel-plated snub-nosed .38 revolver.

"Don't move, don't make a sound," Bolan whispered as he jammed the barrel of the revolver into the fat covering Guzman's ribs.

Guzman froze in place. The sack began to shake.

"I said *don't move,*" Bolan said in a gruffer voice.

"I…can't help it," Guzman whispered back.

Bolan reached out and took the pistachios, dropping them on the seat between them. "Well," he said, "you'd better learn how to help it. Because you've got an acting job facing you, and if you don't pull it off convincingly, you're gonna die on stage. And I don't mean that figuratively."

"Listen, please," Guzman whispered. "I'll give you all of the three million back. Just don't shoot me." He continued to tremble on the other side of the car.

Bolan did another fast 360-degree surveillance of the outside of the car. The armed cartel men were still standing with their backs to him and their leader, and had not picked up on what was going on inside the car. Turning back to Guzman, Bolan said, "We're going to get out of the car, and we're going to act like two best friends who haven't seen each other in years. You're going to tell your men we've worked everything out, and that you and I'll ride in the front car back to your office." Bolan dropped the revolver into the side pocket of his suit coat. "There's no way I can kill six of your men before they get me," he said, "but I can certainly kill *you* if anything goes wrong. So be convincing. Because I'll blow your head off the second before I die if I even suspect you're trying to alert these guys in any way."

Guzman remained frozen.

"Loosen up," Bolan said firmly. "Because I'm not kidding. I'll kill you even if you *are* trying but aren't doing a good job."

The words seemed to snap Guzman back into reality. He

took two deep breaths, then said, "I am as ready as I'm ever going to be."

"That had better be very ready," Bolan reminded him. He wrapped his fingers around the grips of the .38 and kept his finger on the double-action trigger. Then he tapped on the window behind him and the man leaning against the window moved away and opened the door.

Bolan crawled out then reached in with his left hand to help the obese man. His right hand stayed firmly around the grips of the revolver.

Guzman got out, and for the first time Bolan had enough light to get a good look at the man's face. It was flabby like the rest of him, and his skin bore the scars of severe acne from his younger years.

"Tell them," Bolan whispered.

"*Muchachos!*" Guzman shouted, and the word echoed off the walls of the old salt mine. "My American friend and I have come to an agreement. But we must return to my office for a few moments." His eyes moved toward the headlights and he shaded them with his hand. "I will ride with my friend in the car he came in. Pedro—" he glanced toward the man in the white suit "—you and Luis will come with us. The rest of you follow in the other car."

The blond man—Bolan now knew him to be named Pedro—frowned in the shadows. Luis did the same. "Are you sure everything is all right, *jefe?*" Pedro asked. "You look… concerned."

Guzman forced a bright smile in the darkened cave. "*Sí, sí,* everything is all right," he said as he waddled toward the car that had brought Bolan. The Executioner followed, keeping his hand in his pocket as one of the men opened the back door. "Do not worry," Guzman repeated. "My new friend… what is your name?"

"Cooper. Matt Cooper."

"Matt Cooper and I have worked everything out and look

forward to a long and prosperous business arrangement." He
slid into the backseat. Bolan got in next to him.

As Pedro and Luis returned to the front, Bolan angled the
barrel of the .38 toward Guzman and smiled. "Now that we're
such good friends, Eddie," he said, "don't you think your men
could give me back my weapons?"

Guzman closed his eyes, then opened them. "Certainly.
Give them to him."

The Beretta, Desert Eagle, NAA Pug and Cold Steel
Espada were handed over the seat to Bolan. He replaced
the two big guns in their holsters, dropping the Pug into his
right pants pocket since it was no longer serving as a hideout
weapon. The Cold Steel Espada came last, and he slipped it
back in its usual place behind his hip.

The first Mercedes pulled forward and turned around, then
the twin vehicles started out of the salt mine.

19

Eduardo Guzman, Bolan and the men in the other Mercedes got out of the cars in front of an office building in downtown Bogotá.

Bolan, fully armed again, continued to keep his hand in his jacket pocket and wrapped around the cartel boss's .38.

But only Guzman knew that Bolan had turned the tables during their brief private conference in the backseat of the automobile, and that he, rather than the cartel drug runner, was actually calling the shots.

"Bring Luis and Pedro," Bolan whispered into Guzman's ear. "Have one of them get the million-and-a-half out of the other car first. And tell the rest of the men to stay in that other car."

Guzman did as he was told. And while there were several curious looks thrown their way from the men in the other Mercedes, the cartel leader's bodyguards did as they were told.

Guzman's suite of offices were on the first floor of the tall skyscraper, and the fat man waddled toward a door which announced Guzman Imports & Exports. A moment later they were inside the front office and passing an attractive young woman who sat working at a computer.

"Good day, Anita," Guzman said as he led the way past her desk to the door just to her side.

"Good day, Mr. Guzman," the woman said in Spanish, barely looking up.

The four men entered Guzman's private office, and the fat man went directly to the safe behind his desk. Bolan nodded toward it, shifting the revolver in his coat pocket slightly for emphasis.

Guzman saw the movement, but so did Luis and Pedro.

Bolan could see the concerned looks on both men's faces. They could sense that something was wrong, but they weren't sure what.

The odds against the Executioner, however, had dwindled. Instead of facing six men armed with submachine guns and assault rifles and having nothing but his hands to fight them, Bolan had all of his own weapons back, and the two men were reduced to whatever pistols they had hidden under their suits. The soldier had no doubt he could outdraw and kill them both if it came to it. But that would mean a running gunfight all the way from downtown Bogotá to the airport, and facing police and military guards before he and Grimaldi could take off.

The Executioner didn't like those odds any better than he had the earlier ones back at the salt mines. No, he thought, this was still a time for stealth rather than direct action.

At least for as long as he could pull it off.

Bolan let go of Guzman's .38 and removed his hand from his coat pocket. But in the same motion, he casually grasped the lapel of his jacket, ready to draw the sound-suppressed Beretta. If he had to resort to that here, perhaps he could at least keep the noise down so the men outside in the other car didn't hear it.

Guzman struggled onto his knees to work the combination lock on the safe, as Bolan's mind and course of attack shifted gears from the .38 as his first line of attack to the Beretta in his shoulder holster. He studied the faces of Luis and Pedro and saw their concerned looks relax. At least partially.

"Señor Guzman and I are entering into a very large-scale transaction," Bolan told the two men whose expressions were begging an explanation. "We don't have time to tell you the details right now."

Guzman was working the dial on the safe. "But it will mean a very large bonus for you and the men outside," he added on his own accord. His words reminded Bolan that the man was still scared out of his wits and more than willing to play along with the charade.

"If you would, gentlemen," Bolan said as the safe door finally swung open. "Find us several briefcases. Empty some out if need be. We're going to need them."

Luis and Pedro exchanged glances and again their faces looked puzzled. Bolan knew it was only a matter of time before the tension in the room caused one or both of them to start asking questions that couldn't be answered. And he had another logistical problem, if he had to kill the two men inside the office. Even if he could do so with the quiet Beretta, he would have to hide the bodies and call in at least two more of Guzman henchmen to help carry the money from the safe.

Thirty million dollars, even if it was all in hundred-dollar bills, was going to be far too much for two men to carry. Especially if Bolan had to keep his gun hand ready at all times, which he would in case this "good friend" cover went south.

A few minutes later, the money—it had been wrapped with brown paper bands in stacks of ten thousand dollars each—had been transferred to a half-dozen briefcases and other carriers.

But the sight of so much money, and the fact that the safe was suddenly empty, had brought the curious tension back to the faces of Pedro and Luis. "Boss," Luis said, "are you certain this is what you want to do?"

Guzman didn't even have to glance at Bolan to know what

to say. "Who is in charge here?" he demanded in a forced-gruff tone of voice.

"You are, sir," Pedro said quickly.

"Then do as I tell you and do not ask questions."

Luis and Pedro simply nodded.

Lifting the briefcases, the four men strode back out past Anita and through the office building lobby to the twin Mercedes. They loaded the cash in the lead car's trunk and backseat. By the time they were finished, there was barely room for Bolan and Guzman to get in.

"Tell the other car to stay here," Bolan said under his breath to Guzman, and the fat cartel boss turned and gave the order. The look on the faces of the four gunmen in the matching Mercedes-Benz told Bolan they needed to get out of there before the men had too much time to think.

"Let's go," he said quietly again.

"Drive quickly, Pedro," Bolan said as the man returned to the wheel of their vehicle. "There are great things ahead, and we're on a tight time schedule."

But by this point, both Luis and Pedro had witnessed too many "little" things that didn't quite add up. Luis turned in the passenger's seat and said, "Is that correct, boss?"

Guzman glanced at Bolan. Then he said simply, *"Sí."*

As the lone Mercedes made its way out of downtown Bogotá toward the airport, Bolan leaned forward. "You guys need to relax," he said gently. "Señor Guzman and I are working on a deal that's is going to make everybody rich, including you. So bear with us if things seem a little out of the ordinary."

The men in the front seat were no different than most career criminals. They were greedy. And the opportunity for great wealth outweighed their common sense. Just like Bolan had found with most outlaws during his career of fighting them, they believed what they wanted to believe.

Twenty minutes later, the same colonel who had met them

on landing escorted the Mercedes across the airport in his jeep. He stayed in his seat as Luis and Pedro helped Bolan and Guzman load the money onto the Learjet while Jack Grimaldi warmed up the airplane.

"Señor Guzman will be going with us," Bolan told the two henchmen when they'd finished. "Isn't that right, Eduardo?"

"Sí, sí," Guzman said. "Go back and await my orders."

Bolan helped the fat man onto the plane and into the seat right behind the one he would take.

Ten seconds later, the Learjet was racing down the runway and rising into the air.

Guzman didn't speak until they were over Panama.

"Señor Cooper," he finally said, leaning forward to talk to Bolan. "You can keep the money."

"Thank you," the Executioner said. "Of course I was planning to do so anyway."

"Just drop me off somewhere. I have no desire to spend the rest of my life in an American prison." He was sweating profusely by then. "I can get you even more money if you like."

"No, thanks," Bolan said. "I think this'll be enough."

For a moment, a look of hope replaced the fear on Guzman's face. "Then you will not take me back to the U.S. for prosecution?" he said.

The Executioner was about to answer the man when he noticed Guzman reaching behind his back. But before the drug boss could fully retrieve his weapon, Bolan shot him between the eyes with Guzman's own .38. Don Eduardo was officially out of the drug business.

20

Bolan took four million dollars in two of the briefcases and left the rest of the money in the Learjet with Grimaldi. The ace pilot would take it back to Stony Man Farm, and it would go a long way in helping to finance the destruction of other criminal and terrorist organizations around the world.

Bolan stopped at the condo McFarley had provided for him for a moment, picked up a small-but-essential piece of equipment, then drove to the Hotel Lafitte. Greg Kunkle was waiting, chomping at the bit from his time confined in the room, and ready to get back into action in an attempt to show repentance for his past sins.

"You're going to have to stay hidden in the car," Bolan said as they drove toward McFarley's brothel-mansion. "We're coming close to the end game now, and I don't know exactly what McFarley knows about what happened in Bogotá. But my guess is he's been tipped off as to what actually went down, and I don't want anyone inside the house recognizing you."

Kunkle had been disappointed, but he understood.

Bolan wasn't surprised when two new faces—both who looked like they'd taken their share of punches in the boxing ring—met him at the front door of the brothel. They escorted

him up the elevator, then stopped in the hall just outside Mc-
Farley's office.

"We have orders to search you," one of the men said. His
nose seemed to have been knocked permanently to the left
side of his face.

That didn't surprise Bolan, but he felt he had to act like it
did. "I thought we were past all that," he said. "We starting
over again?"

The man with the crooked nose just looked him in the eye.
"Orders are orders," he said.

The fact that they wanted his weapons again before he met
with McFarley told Bolan a good deal about the situation.
Someone from Bogotá—probably one of the guards in the
second Mercedes—had called McFarley and given him the
heads-up that his guy Cooper had killed some of their men
and taken Guzman with him. Something fishy was going on.
And, as always, McFarley was taking no chances.

Bolan knew that Grimaldi's Learjet was fast, but it would
never be able to outrun a phone call or email.

Bolan willingly handed over the Beretta, Desert Eagle,
NAA Pug and the Espada. The two new men had also taken
the two briefcases that contained the four million dollars Mc-
Farley was expecting.

Bolan was ushered past the secretary's desk and into Mc-
Farley's office.

The criminal mastermind sat in his usual place behind his
desk. The only difference was that instead of the gold-plated
nail clipper he usually held in his hand, he gripped the pearl-
handled .455 Webley.

And it was aimed directly at the Executioner.

McFarley didn't waste time. "You're a man of tremendous
talent," he told Bolan. "But every step of the way, every job
I've given you, there's always been some kind of unusual outcome. Always something that had to be explained. One or

two discrepancies I could overlook. But when you put them all together…" His voice trailed off and he shook his head.

"So what's the problem this time?" Bolan asked.

"The problem is, I told you to only take four million dollars from Guzman so we could resume our smuggling arrangement after all this blew over and tempers cooled. Instead, you take his whole thirty million. Thirty million may seem like a lot to you, Cooper, but it's not. Working together, Guzman and I could have made that much every month. But not now. And what's more, you bring me only the four million I asked for. I told you before. I have people watching everyone who works for me."

"I kind of looked at the rest of the money as a bonus for a job well done," Bolan said.

"I might have given you a bonus if you'd brought it all in, but you didn't. So all you're going to get now is a .455-inch round of lead." The Irishman cocked the Webley and kept it aimed at Bolan. "You're just a little too good for your own health," he said.

"So I'll get you the rest of the money and we'll go from there."

"It's not that simple," McFarley grunted. "Word of what happened will get around. You see how fast I learned about it? My firearms connections, the people whose whores I import, everyone I do business with is going to hear about this and treat me like a leper for a while. Nobody will trust me. At least not for a long time."

Bolan's smile grew slightly. "I think you can still live pretty well on what you've got," he said. Casually, he hooked a thumb over his belt buckle.

McFarley slammed his empty hand down on his desk. "That's not the point, you son of a bitch!" he shouted. "I *like* what I do." His whole body was trembling—he was losing control. Bolan knew that it wouldn't be much longer before he pulled the Webley's trigger.

"I like the power!" the Irishman screamed at the top of his lungs.

"Guys like you always do," Bolan said calmly. Then, just as calmly he quickly stepped to the side and drew a second NAA Pug—the one he had picked up from his condo before going to get Kunkle—from behind his belt buckle, cocked the single-action mechanism and sent a .22 Magnum hollowpoint bullet drilling through Tommy McFarley's left eye.

The explosion shocked the two men in the room, and Bolan took advantage of their surprise to cock the tiny firearm again. The man with the crooked nose took his next round in one of his twisted nostrils, and the third man dropped to another shot in the center of his forehead.

The Executioner had known he was likely to be frisked again if word of what he'd done in Colombia had come back to McFarley. And the Pug was too well known within Mc-Farley's circle to be a hideout. But Bolan had gambled that the presence of *two* of the tiny wheel guns would not have crossed the minds of any new, dim-witted punch-drunk lackeys McFarley might have employed in his absence.

And that bet had paid off.

Bolan dropped to one knee, gathering up the other weapons McFarley's two goons had taken from him. Then he walked quickly to where McFarley's corpse still sat in his chair, threw the body unceremoniously to the floor and took a seat at the former kingpin's computer.

A few minutes later, every file on the Irishman's hard drive was on its way to Kurtzman's vast computer network at Stony Man Farm.

Bolan expected there would be enough evidence gathered from them to keep him, Phoenix Force and Able Team busy for a long time.

As soon as the files had been sent, Bolan exited the office and went directly to the elevator. Sugar, dressed in black lingerie, was waiting for him. The women downstairs had obviously heard the shots. But until that moment, they had no idea who had been shot.

Bolan looked at the woman. "You and the girls should find another job, Sugar," he said as they reached the ground floor and Bolan started out of the house. "Preferably in another type of profession. McFarley is out of business."

Kunkle's head popped up from the backseat as Bolan opened the driver's door and got in. The detective's SIG-Sauer was in his hand.

As they drove away from the mansion, Kunkle said, "I don't know what to do now that it's over."

Bolan turned to look at the man. He was one-hundred-percent convinced that Kunkle had truly experienced the life-changing experience he claimed to have had. And nothing was going to change this new man who, the Executioner could sense, would spend the rest of his life doing good.

Unless this same good man was confined to prison.

"You ever kill anybody?" Bolan asked.

"Well, sure, you know I—"

"I meant outside the line of duty. Murder."

"No," Kunkle said. "All I did was take payoffs to turn my head on illegal gambling, a few marijuana runs, and that sort of thing."

"Then I've got an idea for you," Bolan said.

"What's that?" Kunkle asked.

"How about just going back to your job and being an *honest* cop from now on?" the Executioner said.

* * * * *

AleX Archer
LABYRINTH

Solve the puzzle...or die trying.

Abducted by a famous environmental terrorist who is after the Tome of Prossos, Annja Creed is the key to retrieving the ancient manuscript hidden somewhere deep within the mansion of a book dealer. She has only twelve hours to decipher the labyrinth's sinister secret...a secret that could ensure she never emerges.

Available January wherever books are sold.

www.readgoldeagle.blogspot.com

GRA34

James Axler
Outlanders®

PLANET HATE

A self-styled new god hijacks humanity in his quest for ultimate vengeance...

With their greatest asset, archivist Brigid Baptiste, lost to the enemy, Kane and the Cerberus rebels are losing the battle—but not yet the war. As Kane succumbs to incapacitating hallucinations, Brigid's dark avatar lays siege to a special child who is the link to a ghastly pantheon of despotic rule.

Available February wherever books are sold.